FINDING ZOLA

FINDING ZOLA

Marianne Mitchell

Boyds Mills Press

To Mary Beth Englund for her friendship,
inspiration, and counsel.

Text copyright © 2003 by Marianne Mitchell
All rights reserved

Published by Boyds Mills Press, Inc.
A Highlights Company
815 Church Street
Honesdale, Pennsylvania 18431
Printed in China
Visit our Web site at www.boydsmillspress.com

Publisher Cataloging-in-Publication Data (U.S)

Mitchell, Marianne.
    Finding Zola / by Marianne Mitchell. —1st ed.
[144] p. ; cm.
Summary: A thirteen-year-old girl investigates the disappearance of an older woman in
this coming-of-age mystery.
ISBN 1-59078-070-1
1. Detective and mystery stories — Juvenile literature. (1. Mystery and detective stories.)
I.Title.
  [F] 21 AC   2003
2002108408

First edition, 2003
The text of this book is set in 13-point Minion.

10 9 8 7 6 5 4 3 2 1

Chapter 1

THE DREAM HIT ME AGAIN THAT FIRST MORNING in Copper Valley.

I jerked awake, my heart racing. Somewhere in the house, a phone was ringing. I blinked hard, gulping for air like a fish flopping on dry sand. Shaking my head, I tried to sweep away the fragments of that awful dream. I scanned the room, searching for familiar sights. There weren't any. Instead, I faced walls of tan adobe blocks. Wooden shutters covered the windows, letting in a dim morning light. A dove cooed on the window ledge. No, I wasn't in my own bedroom in San Diego. This was Grandma Emilia's townhouse in Arizona.

I glanced at the framed picture on the bedside table. It was a photo of Dad as a teenager with dark ponytailed hair just like mine. He stood holding a garden hose by his Corvette, a silly grin on his face like he was about the turn the hose on whoever was taking the photo. For an instant I thought he even winked at me, as if to say "Hiya, Crystal!" I still couldn't believe he was dead.

I pushed myself up into a sitting position, then carefully lifted my legs over the side of the bed. With my right hand, I grasped the arm of my wheelchair and made the transfer. After a long stop in the bathroom—every little thing took so much time now—I headed out to the patio, where Mom sat reading the paper. Dressed in faded jeans and a sleeveless blouse, she looked more like my sister than my mother. Her short-cropped brown hair always had a casual, windblown look.

"Morning!" said Mom. "How'd you sleep?"

"Lousy. I had that dream again." I reached for the pitcher of orange juice and poured a glass.

Mom put down the paper. "I'm sorry, Cryssy."

"When I woke up, I didn't know where I was."

"Smack dab in the middle of the desert. Don't worry, we won't be here long."

"Good."

It had been a year since the accident that had killed my dad and left me in a wheelchair. Even after six months of physical therapy, I still had no movement from the waist down. It had also cost me a year of school. Next fall, at thirteen, I'd only be a seventh-grader. Going back to school was not something I was looking forward to. When I show up in a wheelchair, everyone will look at me like I'm a freak.

"Did the phone ring?" I asked, taking a bite from a muffin.

"Yes. It was Dora McIntyre from the Archuleta Gallery in Santa Fe. The good news is, someone canceled out of an exhibit. She asked if I'd mind stepping in at the last minute and showing my work. Of course, I said I'd be glad to. Imagine, Santa Fe!"

"Cool. What's the bad news?"

"The bad news is, I have to leave tomorrow. For a week."

"But we just got here! Have you seen how much stuff Gran had?"

"I know, I know. But all that 'stuff' isn't going anywhere. We can take our time sorting through it."

I leaned back in my chair and closed my eyes. First I lost Dad, then Gran died. Now we had to pack up her things and sell her townhouse. My life seemed full of "never agains." Gran and I would never again sit on the patio and tell each other stories. I'd never again hear her laugh or hold her soft, wrinkly hand. Maybe she and Dad were up in Heaven right now, watching over us. A sigh hiccuped out of me. My eyes blurred with tears.

Overhead, wind chimes tinkled in the morning breeze, as if Gran was trying to send us a comforting song.

"I miss her. I miss her voice, her stories, her 'wise' sayings."

Mom smiled and nodded. "Me, too. Those proverbs just seemed to grow on the tip of her tongue."

Whenever I'd wish things would go faster, Gran would tug on my hair and tease me, saying, *"Paciencia, pioja."* Patience, little louse. She'd often leave out the other half of the proverb: *que la noche es larga.* The night is long. I was always rushing into things without thinking first. Those proverbs were her way of teaching me a little from the Mexican side of my family. Dad had grown up hearing Spanish from his parents. Mom's side was Irish, so what Spanish I knew I got from Dad or Gran.

Mom started stacking the breakfast dishes on a tray. "I'd better get busy. I've got to figure out which paintings to take."

I let the news of Mom's trip sink in. She'd been hoping to get a show in Santa Fe for a long time. It was a shot at the Big Time—a chance to hang her paintings next to some famous artist's. Maybe someday my mom, Sandra O'Connell Ramos, would be famous, too.

"How long will you be gone?" I asked.

"Dora said it would take a couple of days to set everything up. Then four days to meet and greet the public. A day to drive there and a day back. Eight days, max."

"Well, don't worry about me. I'll have lots of Gran's things sorted and boxed by the time you get back. I'll be fine by myself."

Mom shook her head.

"Why not?" I protested. "I can take care of myself."

"I know you can, Cryssy. But I can't leave you here alone for a week. You don't drive, you aren't used to a gas stove—"

"I'll order pizza!"

"And you'd be lonesome! This town is not exactly full of kids your age, remember?"

That stopped me. This was Geezer City, all right. The average age was probably seventy-five. In most neighborhoods, you couldn't even buy a house unless one of the buyers was sixty. You couldn't have kids under eighteen living with you, either. I was glad Gran had chosen one of the nonrestricted neighborhoods. "I don't want to be stuck with just *los viejos*," she'd said.

"So . . ." Mom continued, "I asked Gran's neighbor, Zola, to come over and stay with you."

I groaned. Just what I needed—an eighty-year-old baby sitter. "Why her?"

"For one thing, I trust her. Zola practically lived over here while Gran was sick. She took care of her right up to the end. You know how hard it was on me to live six hours away and constantly worry about Gran. I don't know what we would have done without Zola's help."

It was all true. Mom had wanted to come more often, but she was teaching an art class and I was still recovering. Even so, Mom called Gran nearly every day, offering to come. But Gran kept putting her off, saying she didn't want to be a burden and that she was pampered enough already by her neighbor.

I put the basket of muffins on my lap and followed Mom inside. I was really happy she was getting a chance to show her paintings. Santa Fe was known all over the country as an art center. She should do it. But leave me stuck with Zola? I'd only met her once, about a year ago, just before my accident. All I remembered about her was that she seemed old. And a little odd.

"What about DJ? Could she come down?"

Mom thought for a moment. "That's a great idea. The semester's over by now. I'll give her a call."

That made me feel better. DJ—she never used her real name, Dolores Josefina—was my cousin. She was a sophomore at the University of Arizona and a star player on their girls' softball team. I hadn't seen much of her lately, but we used to be pretty close. Before the accident, that is.

Everything in my life had fallen on two sides: Before Accident and After Accident. Before the accident, I never thought about what I could or couldn't do. I just did it. Sometimes, like Gran loved to remind me, I got in over my head without thinking first about the consequences. The accident sure knocked that out of me. Now I found myself holding back, afraid to try things. I didn't like it at all. I wanted the old me back.

Gran had another favorite saying for me whenever I got discouraged. *Donde una puerta se cierra, otra se abre.* Where one door closes, another one opens. She was right. I was deep into a crossword puzzle that morning when someone started pounding on the front door.

Chapter 2

THE SUDDEN NOISE STARTLED ME. When I opened the door, a disheveled old lady stood there, her frizzy gray hair poofed out around her face like a halo. She wore floppy bedroom slippers and a pale blue housedress that was buttoned all wrong. She bent forward and shouted at me.

"I am late?"

I sat there blinking for a minute, wondering if the woman thought that because I was in a wheelchair, I must be deaf, too.

"Zola?"

"Yes. I am Zola. Who are you?"

"Crystal. My mother's expecting you."

Zola edged right by me and into the house like she owned the place. "Yes, yes. I come over to Emilia's. So sad about her. Bring her soup. Bring her flowers. Give bath. Such a sweet lady. You knew her?" Her knobby fingers fussed with the top button on her dress that had missed its hole.

"Yes. She was my grandmother."

"So, Sandra calls and I come." Zola padded down the hallway, not waiting for directions or formalities. She had a deep voice that reminded me of a Russian spy from old movies. All her *esses* sounded like *zees*. *Zo, Zandra callz* . . .

I shook my head, wondering what possessed Mom to ask a Russian spy to stay with me. I shut the door and pushed my way after Zola. "She can't be serious," I muttered to myself. "She can't do this to me!"

In the back bedroom Mom sat in the middle of the floor, putting the last bit of masking tape on several square packages wrapped in brown paper. She looked up as Zola came marching in.

"Zola!" Mom stood up, wiped her hands on the back of her faded blue jeans, and took Zola's small hand. "Thanks for agreeing to stay with Crystal on such short notice."

"Is no problem." Zola gazed around the room and sighed. "So sad. I am here every day for Emilia. Is hard to believe she is gone."

Patting Zola's arm, Mom said, "You were a big help. With us living in San Diego, it eased our minds knowing Gran had a friend like you to look in on her."

Zola's head bobbed in agreement. "She was fine lady. Someday I hope someone is looking after me." She pointed to the packages on the floor. "You are leaving soon?"

"Yes, first thing in the morning," said Mom. "I've got six paintings wrapped, strapped, and ready to go! I'll call as soon as I get to Santa Fe. I left the number where I can be reached by the phone."

"Then I go home to pack my things." Zola turned to me, her pale eyes crinkling and her hands scratching playfully at the air. "I come back in morning. We have good time, yes?"

"Umm, yeah. Sure," I mumbled, watching her head back down the hall. I sat there for a few moments, picking at the padding on my armrests, picturing me and Zola having a such a "good time" playing pinochle. Or cleaning moldy cheese out of the refrigerator. Or watching the birds poop on the back patio.

"Mom, does she have to stay here with me? She seems . . . I don't know, spacey. Like she's got a few files missing. She didn't even know who I was when I answered the door."

"She's only met you once, remember. Look, she knows this house and how to take care of the ones who live here. She's already proven herself. Besides, I think it helps her to feel useful to others."

I wrinkled my nose. "I feel like a charity case."

"Be happy, Crystal. It's only for a week. Plus, I called DJ and she's coming down in the morning." Mom gathered up the paintings, placing two on my lap. "Come on. You can carry these for me."

I followed Mom out to the carport. I noticed a small travel bag in the back seat of the car.

"You didn't waste any time getting ready, did you?"

She smiled at me, bending down to give me a hug. "Cryssy, I've been getting ready for a show like this for twenty years! This could make a big difference in our lives. You know how tight money has been."

"I thought you'd take more paintings."

"Dora already has five at the gallery. I had planned on taking all the paintings I gave Gran, but I can't find one of them."

"Which one?"

"It's one I did years ago of your father working on a sculpture. It was called *David and Goliath*. I remember how pleased Gran was to get it. She even had a special frame made for it. Very fancy. Silver with turquoise inlay."

"I remember that painting."

"Gran kept it right over her bed. Only now it's missing." Mom shut the trunk of the car, looking pensive. "Why on earth would she have taken it down?"

Chapter 3

As I watched Mom drive off the next morning, I felt a twinge of excitement. I had a whole week ahead of me to stretch my wings. Oh, sure, old Zola would be here, but I wasn't going to let her stop me from trying a few things. Maybe DJ and I could go shopping. Nogales was only thirty miles to the south. We could even practice bargaining in Spanish. But first I wanted to start packing some of Gran's stuff.

In the kitchen I found a stack of old newspapers, perfect for wrapping dishes. Then I headed down the hall to Mom's room. I knew she'd left more cardboard boxes and some tape piled up in the corner. After nesting four of the boxes together and piling them on my lap along with the roll of tape, I pushed my way back down the hall to the living room. When I got near my room, I thought I saw a flickering light. It had that pale blue glow of a television. That's odd, I thought. There's no TV in my room. As I went through the door, I felt the hair on the back of my neck prickle. The room felt as cold as a freezer.

Over by the bedside table, Dad's picture sat in a halo of blue light. The light pulsed once and went out. I jerked in surprise, knocking the roll of tape off my lap and sending it under one of the twin beds. Tilting my head, I peered down as best I could to find it. It had come to a stop by a bundle wrapped in a towel. I leaned down, trying to grab the tape, but it was too far under and I nearly tumbled out of my chair. There was no way I could get to it. What bothered me more was the weird blue light. What was *that* all about? I shrugged it off, deciding it must have been sunlight coming in at a funny angle.

By eleven that morning, Zola still hadn't come over. At first I didn't mind. I was enjoying being on my own, puttering around. But she had told Mom she'd be over in the morning. So where was she? On my way into the kitchen, I peered out the front window. Zola's townhouse sat directly across from Gran's. There she was, all right, sweeping something out her front door. Water dribbled down her driveway. Why was Zola sweeping water out of her house?

It took me less than a minute to wheel across the street. She looked up, her blue eyes bulging in panic. "Water all over my house! Come!"

Inside, the floor plan was exactly like Gran's, only backwards. A small entry opened to a combined living room and dining area. To the left was a small kitchen. To the right, a hallway led to bedrooms and the bath.

Zola waved her arms. "Water, everywhere!"

Sure enough, water pooled over the whole tiled floor. From somewhere down the hall, I heard splashing. I eased through the puddles toward the bathroom. There, water thundered into an already full tub, sloshing over the sides like a waterfall.

"You left your bath running!" I shouted.

Zola came in, shook her head, and turned the knobs to off. Then she stood up, her shoulders drooping in confusion. "I am eating breakfast. I go into the bathroom. But then I get here and I forget why." She cocked her worried face toward me. "Who are you?"

Weird. She seemed to have no memory of meeting me. It was like it had never happened. I wondered if she'd also forgotten her promise to come stay with me.

"I'm Crystal, from across the street. You came over to Gran's house yesterday. Don't you remember?"

"Oh, yes. Emilia's house. How is Emilia?" She didn't wait for an answer. Instead she splashed back down the hall, muttering to herself.

I sat there, stunned. Oh, great. This is just great. Mom has hired a crazy, forgetful old lady to take care of me. I followed Zola back to the kitchen. She sat at the small table, spreading red jelly on a piece of toast.

"You want toast?" she asked, like nothing was wrong.

"No, thank you."

She pointed to my wheelchair. "Why you are in that thing?"

"I was in a car accident." *Please don't ask any more,* I begged silently. I hated talking about the accident. So I changed the subject. "Do you live here by yourself?"

Zola chuckled. "Yes. One brother in Chicago. But he is old and crazy. Not smart, like me!"

Mom had told me that the neighborhood association provided upkeep and maintenance for the residents. Someone would have to come over here and mop up the water. It shouldn't take too long, since Zola's floors were all done in tile.

Zola looked out the window. "You live over there now?"

"No. We're just packing up Gran's things."

"Yes, the lady who makes the jelly. Jelly from cactus! Taste some. Is good!" She shoved her toast at me.

As I took a bite, a sweetness filled my mouth and a warm glow spread over me. Gran had made this jelly. It brought her back, if only for a moment.

"I know lady who makes the jelly," Zola repeated,

"from those ugly cactus." She pointed out the window.

I stared across the street. Clumps of gray-green prickly pear cactus filled Gran's front yard. Stubs of fruit grew along the edges of the cactus pads. Come August they'd ripen, full of blood-red juice.

"Zola, do you remember talking with my mother? About you coming to stay with me? Mom left this morning for Santa Fe. Remember?"

She sat there a moment, thinking. Then, as if a light had gone on inside, she nodded. "Yes. Now I remember. You are Crystal." She reached out and patted my hand. "My mind—it is so forgetful. I don't know what is happening to me."

Suddenly, she looked so small and frail. Her eyes glistened with tears, and worry creased her face. I thought of how often I'd wished I could forget things, especially bad memories. Now I was looking into the face of someone who was very frightened about forgetting.

"It's okay, Zola. We all forget sometimes. I'll help you get your stuff together and we'll go over to Gran's house. I'll call someone to come clean up the water."

We went back to her bedroom and she collected a few things in an overnight case. From her closet, she took out a frilly pink dress and held it up.

"Wednesday I go to dance class." She flashed me a bright smile, her eyes crinkling with excitement. "I look pretty, no?"

While Zola packed, I tried to imagine her flitting around on the dance floor. After all, she hadn't always been an old lady. On her dresser were photos of a younger, more adventurous Zola riding horseback in the mountains, standing on the Great Wall of China, shooting a rifle at a target. I guess she'd had a Before time, too, just like me.

When we headed out the door, I noticed the empty carport. "How will you get to your dance class?"

"Taxi come. Always the taxi." She stomped into the street, looked toward town, and shook her fist. "I sell car when they take away my driving license. Is not right! Why they do that?"

"So you won't kill anyone, you old fool!" a man shouted back at her.

I turned my head and stared at the man in the next driveway. He was dressed in white slacks and a knit top, and had just plunked a bag of clubs into his golf cart. His pure white hair made a striking contrast with his dark, tanned skin. A boy about my age sat waiting in the cart.

"Oh, go away!" snapped Zola.

"You should be in a nursing home, where you couldn't get into trouble!" The man hopped in the cart and pulled into the street, jerking to a stop a few feet from us. "Don't you go bothering that poor girl with your problems," he huffed, nodding toward me.

What a jerk! I thought. He sat there, looking smug

and picking on an old lady. I strained to get a look at the boy seated next to him. He wore shorts and a T-shirt, but a blue golf cap hid his face. He kept his head down, as if he didn't want any part of this little scene. The older man gave a snort and drove off.

Zola sighed, her shoulders sagging. "He is idiot! Big lawyer idiot!"

"Ignore him," I said. "I don't mind helping you out while I'm here."

She placed her hand on my head and stroked it. "You are good girl."

"I have an idea. My cousin DJ is coming soon from Tucson. Why don't we all go out for lunch and get pizza?"

Her face lit up. "Yes! Is good! But first I fix up house."

"Let the maintenance men do that, Zola. We'll come to pick you up about noon."

Zola paused, looking back at her house. "No. Better go at six. I do important job first."

"Can I help?"

"No, no. Something I do by myself." She gave me a wink and headed back into her house, still carrying her overnight case. She turned at the door and put her finger to her lips. "Is top secret!"

I tried not to laugh as I headed back across the street. Maybe my first guess about Zola had been right. Maybe she really was a spy.

Chapter 4

FIRST I CALLED THE MAINTENANCE OFFICE and asked them to send someone to clean up the mess at Zola's house. While I waited for DJ, I started checking Gran's cupboards and closets, wondering what we could get rid of and what we should keep. It would take a while to sort through it all. Part of me said I should be asking Gran's permission to do this. The rest of me felt her spirit right next to me saying, "It's all right, *mi amor*. These things aren't mine anymore."

Most of Gran's furniture was old, dumpy stuff she'd had for years. Mom would probably donate the olive green overstuffed chairs and sofa to the Salvation Army.

Her heavy bedroom furniture, too. We sure couldn't move it. There was only one piece in the living room I wanted to keep—her knickknack shelf and all its little treasures. As a kid, while my parents and Gran visited, I used to play for hours with the miniature tea set and the Mexican figurines of turtles, birds, and rabbits.

When DJ's turquoise convertible pulled into the carport, nervous doubts about seeing her kicked in. I wondered if she was going to act differently toward me, After Accident and all. I watched as she grabbed a duffel bag from the back seat and headed for the door. She looked great—tan and slim, her movements smooth and sure.

"*¡Hola, chica!* Long time no see," she said, stepping inside. Grinning, she pushed her sunglasses up on top of her head. Her dark hair was slicked back into a tight French braid. She had on a gray Arizona T-shirt that matched her gym shorts, both with red Wildcat logos.

"Hi. Glad you could come," I said. As I closed the door, I was relieved to see a panel truck parked in front of Zola's. Good, I thought. The maintenance men will keep that poor old lady from spending her day mopping floors.

I glanced down at DJ's bag. "Is that all you brought?"

She patted her duffel. "The team travels so much that I've learned to pack light. Brought a swimsuit, though. This place has a pool, doesn't it?"

"Yeah. It's not far. We'll walk over there in a while."

Her eyes flitted briefly to my chair.

Uh-oh. Here we go. "I know what you're thinking," I said. "How can she talk about walking? Right?"

"Well, I—"

"I say 'go for a walk' all the time. Sounds better than 'go for a roll,' don't you think?"

She smiled, giving my chair a friendly nudge. "It must be hard getting around and all."

"I manage. Come on, you can put your things in my room. It has twin beds."

DJ didn't seem too put off by my situation, so I began to relax. She was taking things in stride better than most.

While she unpacked, I brought her up to date on Mom's trip and my "sitter." I wanted to prepare her for spending time with someone who I thought was just dancing around the edges of sanity. From what I'd seen already, I wasn't sure what to expect next from Zola.

"Does she have Alzheimer's?" DJ asked.

"I don't know, Deej. She seemed okay when she was taking care of Gran. She and Mom talked lots on the phone about how things were going. I'm sure Mom thought it was a good idea to have her come over. But maybe she's had a stroke or something."

"Are you going to call your mom and tell her?"

"I thought about it. But this show means too much to her. And now that you're here . . ." I wouldn't say it out loud, but I was really glad to have DJ around. At least she had a car.

"Put your swimsuit on," I said. "I'll show you the pool."

The afternoon heat was cooking full blast, sending the lizards scurrying down holes and under plants to find some shade. I plopped on a hat and led the way down the driveway. We'd only gone a few steps when I felt DJ grab the handles of my chair.

"Hey, you don't have to push. I need the exercise."

She let go. "Oh. Sorry."

"My legs may not work, but my arms are strong. Watch this!" I tilted my chair back and spun around on the wheels, making DJ jump away.

"Careful!"

"Relax. It's good practice for getting over thresholds." I didn't tell her how much I hated it when someone grabbed the chair and tried to push. People thought they were helping when they did that. But if I didn't use my arms, I'd be worse off. Because I had to wheel myself around, my arms and shoulders were stronger than most. Being able to move under my own power meant staying in control. No one was going to take that away!

Next door to Zola's, a man and a woman were loading boxes into their white van. They nodded hello as we passed.

"That's us in a couple of days, loading up Gran's stuff," said DJ.

The pool and cabana were just around the corner. A chainlink fence and oleander hedges separated the pool from the nearby houses. Palm trees fluttered in a hot breeze that reeked of chlorine. The cabana consisted mainly of a covered patio, two bathrooms, and two soda machines tucked into a little alcove. I was surprised no one was swimming on such a hot day.

DJ rubbed her hands together. "Cannonballs, here I come!" She glanced down at me. "Can you still swim?"

I hesitated. "I . . . I don't really know."

By the pool, a huge sign hung on the gate. It read: POOL CLOSED UNTIL FURTHER NOTICE.

"No fair!" cried DJ. "Look at it. Cool, clear water, just begging for someone to jump in and splash around. What gives?"

"It doesn't look polluted or anything. Let's go ask those people loading boxes. Maybe they know why it's closed."

As we walked back, I hid my relief that the pool was closed. Now I wouldn't have to come up with excuses for not going in. I wouldn't have to admit how much water scared me.

They had tried to give me water therapy in rehab, but I panicked every time, so they finally gave up. During the accident, our Jeep had tumbled into a ravine, coming to rest in a small stream. The water had coursed through the wreckage, soaking both Dad and me. It must have been ice cold, but I just felt numb. I remember staring as the current tugged at my jeans. Why couldn't I feel its pull? My whole lower body seemed disconnected from the rest of me. It wasn't until later, in the hospital, that I'd heard the verdict. Paralysis. Damaged spinal cord. No cure.

Nope, swimming pools didn't tempt me at all. With no way to kick or tread water, what would keep me from sinking right to the bottom?

The neighbors were still loading their van. The man reminded me of a summer Santa Claus, with his big round belly and red-and-white shorts. A halo of white hair ringed his head, matching a shaggy white mustache.

"Are you moving?" I asked.

He looked up, startled, then set down the box. "Heavens, no! We're heading up to the swap meet in Tucson."

I explained who we were.

He held out a fleshy hand and gave me a gentle hand-shake. "We wondered who was over there. I'm Ward Tucker." He turned and waved his wife over. "Susan, come here and meet Emilia's granddaughters."

Susan Tucker stood up from taping a box closed, wiping her hands on a trim waist. Her skin was smooth and tan, making her look years younger than her husband. I'd bet anything she paid some plastic surgeon a bundle of money. She held out her hand to me. "Nice to meet you."

"Hi. I'm Crystal. This is my cousin, DJ. We just came

from the pool. How come it's closed?"

Mrs. Tucker smoothed back a stray blond curl and arched her eyebrows. "Closed? No wonder it's been so quiet lately. We usually hear all the splashing and chattering from there. Our rear patio backs up to the pool fence, you know."

"It's all that lawyer's fault," Mr. Tucker said, jerking his head up the street.

"You mean the guy next door to Zola?" I asked.

"That's him. Horace Andrews. Horrible Horace, we call him. He causes some kind of ruckus at every home-owners' meeting. Last week he made a big stink about our insurance rates. Says we need a lifeguard."

"He wasn't very nice to Zola today, either," I added.

Mrs. Tucker shook her head. "That poor lady. Sweet as they come."

"Don't believe everything old Zola tells you, though," Mr. Tucker said as he hoisted another box into the back of the van. "She's over eighty, and she gets things mixed up."

"So I've noticed!"

DJ eyed the last box on the driveway. "Got any pots and pans for sale there? I could use some for my new apartment."

Mr. Tucker shook his head. "Nope. Just a lot of old junk we wanted to get rid of."

"When you live in a place as long as we have, you can

hardly turn around after a while," added Mrs. Tucker.

I glanced over at Gran's house and sighed. "Yeah. We've got a job just like this waiting for us. Come on, Deej. Let's get started. We can get a lot done before we pick up Zola."

Chapter 5

AT A LITTLE BEFORE SIX, I pushed myself out of my wheelchair and slid into the front seat of DJ's car. She folded the chair and wedged it in the back seat, next to some sacks of cans and glass jars we'd packed up to recycle.

"I'll go get Zola," she said.

As she jogged across the street, I noticed how smoothly she moved. Softball training had given her good strong legs. I ran my hand over my own skinny, dead legs. *Stop it, stop it,* I told myself. Things could always be worse. DJ acted pretty normal around me, all in all.

While I waited, I scanned the neighborhood. The townhouses, or casitas, were built so close together that they shared walls and driveways. Gran used to say she liked having people nearby to keep an eye on her. I looked back at Zola's house. DJ was still standing outside the door. What was taking so long? Maybe Zola wasn't ready yet. I fanned myself with a road map, wishing she'd hurry. DJ stepped from the door to the front window and peered in. Then she moved to the other windows, tapping on the glass as she did. She came back alone.

"She's not there. I knocked. I rang. I even peeked in the windows, in case she hadn't heard me. *Nada*."

"Could she have misunderstood?"

"Maybe she forgot all about our dinner date."

I stared down the street and frowned. The Tuckers' van was gone, so we couldn't ask them if they had seen Zola. "Where would she go?" I wondered. "She doesn't have a car. And she seemed so excited about going out for pizza."

"Let's go up to the shopping center and look around. We have to stop at the recycle bins anyway. Maybe she walked up to the pizza place by herself."

The Copper Valley Shopping Center was only a few blocks away, a couple of streets beyond the neighborhood. It was an easy walk if you didn't mind the heat. But the idea of Zola trudging along the hot pavement didn't make much sense. We cruised the parking lot, then pulled into a space outside the Safeway. After dumping the bags in the recycle bins, DJ went into the store.

While I waited, I watched the entrances to the other shops, checking who came and went. Then I recognized someone coming across the parking lot—Zola's grouchy neighbor. I waved at him, beckoning him to come closer. He looked puzzled as he approached.

"We met earlier. I'm looking for your neighbor, Zola. Have you seen her?"

He peered into the window. "Thought you looked familiar." He stuck his hand toward me. "Horace Andrews is the name."

"I'm Crystal. Umm . . . have you seen your neighbor?"

"Not lately. What's that crazy dame done now?"

"My cousin and I were supposed to take her out for pizza. But when DJ knocked at her door, she was gone."

He sighed and looked at the sky. "That woman! Once, she decided to go for a walk but forgot how to get home. She was wandering down the interstate when the highway patrol picked her up. She was so addled she couldn't explain where she lived. It took them half a day to sort it out."

"Could she have done that this time?"

"Who knows?" he said, shrugging his shoulders. "She has no business living alone. She should be in a nursing home where someone can keep track of her. I'll take it up at our next homeowners meeting and—"

DJ thumped on the hood. "No luck. I'll try the drug store."

I bit my lip, thinking. "I'm worried about her, Mr. Andrews. She may be a bit confused, and I'd hate to think she was lost out there somewhere."

He turned to go. "Don't worry. She'll turn up. I'll keep an eye out for buzzards."

As he headed back to his car, I hoped I never had a neighbor like him.

DJ came back with no news. "C'mon," she said. "I'm starved. Let's hit the Pizza Pub. Zola's probably sitting there, wondering where we are."

The smells of garlic and baked bread hit us as soon as we walked in. While DJ went up front to order a pepperoni and sausage pizza, I pushed my chair between the tables and booths, peering at each customer. No Zola.

Part of me said nothing was wrong. She'd just forgotten about us. But a small voice in my head kept muttering, "Not good! Not good!"

While we waited for our order, we tossed around ideas.

"Maybe she got a call from a friend who came to take her out," suggested DJ.

"Why would she go? She seemed so happy about going out for dinner."

"Maybe she just wandered off, like Mr. Andrews said."

I stared out the window. It was seven o'clock, and it was still hot as blazes outside. "That's even worse. Where could she be? And how long has she been gone?"

They called our order number. When DJ brought the pizza back, she said, "Look, there's nothing we can do right now. Let's see if she turns up in the morning."

While we ate, my imagination flashed one question after another. I'd already seen the way Zola got confused. Maybe that was all there was to it. But time was slipping by fast. The desert in the dead of summer was no place to be lost.

When we got home, the message light was flashing on the answering machine.

"Zola, you think?" I pushed the play button. Mom's voice boomed out.

"Hi, Cryssy. I made it here safe and sound. Sorry I missed you. Hope you and DJ are having fun. I'll call tomorrow. Sweet dreams!"

As it turned out, my dreams were anything but sweet.

Chapter 6

A GHOST-WHITE JEEP HURTLED *along the narrow dirt road, taking the corners fast. A girl stared out the window at the canyon below. Jagged rocks pointed accusing fingers at her. Something—a deer, maybe—flashed up ahead and darted across the road. The driver swerved, the wheels spinning as the gravel shoulder gave way. For a moment, time hovered, like the Jeep, with nothing but air and canyon below. The girl gasped, sucking all sounds inside her. Then a scream poured out, echoing off the canyon walls and mixing with the thundering crunch of metal.*

As the dream faded, I woke to voices outside in the street. I glanced at the clock. It was 3:10 in the morning.

Someone was out there. I was sure of it. My heart raced as I pushed myself up. I tried to peek out the window, but the shutters blocked my view. A car door slammed. An engine revved, then the car tore down the street. Who would be out at this hour? Even the paper delivery didn't come this early.

I glanced over at DJ's bed. Soft snoring told me she hadn't heard a thing. I lay back, trying to think of logical reasons for people to be out and about in the middle of the night. I couldn't think of any, especially in a sleepy retirement town like this one.

Wide awake and nervous, I never got back to sleep. When I finally saw daylight seep into the room and heard the doves start to coo, I got up. As I struggled into my slacks, I tried to be quiet and not wake DJ. The first thing I had to do was to see if Zola had come back on her own. A panicky thought hit me. What if that car I heard was someone bringing her back? What if they dropped her off and our door was locked? Would she have found her way to her own house? Now I felt awful that I hadn't gotten up to check. I was sure no one had rung our doorbell. But then again, maybe she had a key.

I peeked into Gran's bedroom but found no sign of Zola. Since she hadn't come back here, I hoped she was in her own house. Trying not to make any noise, I eased my chair out the front door and into the carport.

The air outside echoed with a chorus of quail, doves,

and cactus wrens. It sounded more like a rain forest than a desert, as if the birds were celebrating a few minutes of coolness before the summer heat cranked up. A cottontail rabbit sprinted across the road, his white tail puff disappearing under a bush. For a brief moment, my dark mood lifted.

Across the street, Zola's house sat dead quiet. No lights were on inside. Nothing moved. At the front door, I hesitated. What if Zola was home, sleeping peacefully in her own bed? What right did I have to bother her? I brushed those worries aside. If she got mad, she got mad. I didn't care. At least I'd know she was all right. I reached up and pressed the doorbell. It buzzed like a trapped bee.

After a couple of minutes, I tried again. Nothing. I tried the doorknob. It turned, so I shoved open the door, calling into the stillness. "Zola? Are you here? Hel-lo-o!"

Tilting my wheelchair across the threshold, I pushed into the darkened house. It smelled damp and musty, even though most of the water had dried up. Dining and living room chairs were pushed aside, and towels lay scattered on the floor. Why hadn't the maintenance men finished cleaning up the mess? Zola's pink dancing dress lay in a lump across the sofa. Sitting wide open next to it was a huge black purse, the kind with lots of zippers and pockets. I called out again, louder this time.

"ZOLA!"

No reply.

I pushed hard down the hall to the bedrooms. A quick

check confirmed that Zola wasn't there. She probably hadn't been home all night. Her bed wasn't even rumpled. Where was she? Snatches of her voice echoed in my head. A mix of panic and dread washed over me. I had a sick feeling that things were definitely Not Right.

I hurried outside again, but I didn't lock the door in case she came home. Across the street, DJ was picking up the morning paper on our driveway.

"Where were you?" DJ called. "I thought maybe you'd run off, too."

"She's still gone, Deej. We've got to call the police."

She tucked the paper under her arm. "Don't we have to wait twenty-four hours?"

"But she could be hurt! She's a frail old lady who shouldn't be out wandering around in the heat."

"Look, isn't there a relative you could call? She isn't even related to us."

"She mentioned a brother in Chicago. But I don't know his name or how to reach him."

DJ glanced up the street. "Maybe the neighbors saw something. We should find out more before we call the cops in."

As we headed back inside, I felt the worry building up in my chest. I barely knew Zola, and yet I was connected to her because she had taken care of Gran. It was too early to start knocking on doors, asking questions. "Let's have breakfast," I said. "I can't think on an empty stomach."

DJ whipped up a plate of scrambled eggs, adding glops of salsa on the side. While we ate, I pored over the morning paper, hoping I woudn't find some news story about something that had happened to a lost old lady.

"Think we should call your mom?" mumbled DJ, her mouth full. "She might know more about Zola."

"Uh-uh. She'd only come running back to take care of me. We can handle this." In a way, this was just the challenge I needed to prove I could "rise to the occasion," as Mom liked to say. It had been a while since I'd done anything daring, and I kind of liked the rush I was feeling.

DJ grabbed a section of the paper and groaned. "Aww, gee, two kids were killed in a wreck on I-19."

I flipped through more pages. "A trailer fire. A car-jacking at Tucson Mall. A bunch of house robberies."

"Hey! The Diamondbacks beat the Cubbies!"

"Deej! We're looking for Zola!"

She folded the paper. "Nada. No missing person. No unidentified hit-and-runs. No Jane Doe murders."

I glanced out the front window. "Somebody around here has to have seen something. It's time to start asking questions."

Chapter 7

IN THIS COMPACT NEIGHBORHOOD, the houses hugged each other. Windows looked into other windows. Watching people come and go had to be a major pastime here. When I used to visit Gran, she was always up on what everyone was doing. It was like having live TV right outside.

Our first stop was at Mr. Andrews's door. The kid I'd seen in the golf cart opened it. Now that I got a good look at him, I decided that he was definitely cute. His brown eyes brightened when he saw us.

"Hey, I was just about to come visit you guys," he said. That surprised me. "You were?"

"Yeah. It's boring here with my dad. I was hoping we could, you know, do something."

"Horace Andrews is your dad?"

He shrugged. "Everyone thinks he's my granddad because he's so old. My mom's a lot younger. They're divorced." He stuck his hands deep in his jeans pocket as he talked. "By the way, my name's Matt."

"I'm Crystal. And this is my cousin, DJ."

"I heard about your grandmother. Sorry she died." He glanced down at the ground. He had the longest eyelashes I'd ever seen.

"Thanks," I said. "We're just here long enough to pack up her things and sell the townhouse."

"I'm only here for another week," Matt said. "My mom and I live in Phoenix."

DJ piped in. "We were wondering about your neighbor, Zola. She seems to be missing."

"Dad said you were looking for her last night."

"How come he doesn't like her?" I asked.

Matt shrugged again. "It's not that he doesn't like her, exactly. He thinks she's . . . you know, nuts. He can be kind of rude around old folks. He doesn't realize that he's getting old, too. It's embarrassing."

"So you guys don't know where Zola might be?" DJ asked.

"Uh-uh. But I'll ask him when he gets back from the golf course."

He started to go back inside, but stopped. "Is it okay if I come over sometime? We could do something, like go to the mall or a movie."

"Sure," I said, hoping I didn't sound too eager. "How about tonight?"

He wrinkled his nose, making his freckles wiggle. "Can't tonight. My Dad's got me enrolled in this lapidary class. You know, stone polishing and all? Maybe tomorrow. Good luck with Zola." He ducked his head and slipped inside.

I turned my chair around and studied the other houses on the street. The house to the right of Gran's was vacant, with a red-and-white "sale pending" sign stuck in the dirt. It looked as if no one had lived there for a while. A couple of sun-yellowed newspapers lay forgotten on the driveway. No one to ask over there.

The neighbor on the other side of Gran's was using a hoe to hack out a clump of mistletoe from a palo verde tree. She was trim, with the no-nonsense look of a P.E. teacher. As we approached, she stopped and wiped her sweaty brow.

"Darn mistletoe. If I don't get it out of the trees, they'll die. I'll probably have to saw the whole branch off." She pulled off her glove and shook my hand. Her grip was firm and warm. "I'm Anna Norberg. I saw you and your mother arrive. So sorry about your grandmother. She was a nice lady."

I nodded. "Thanks."

DJ turned and pointed across the street. "Have you seen your neighbor from over there lately?"

Anna Norberg's smile faded. "Zola? Poor lost lady. I don't know how much longer she can go on living on her own."

I leaned forward. "Lost is just the problem. My cousin and I were going to take her out for dinner yesterday. But when we went to pick her up, she was gone. I checked her house this morning and she's still not there."

"Gone? Again?" She cast an anxious glance toward Zola's house. "I'm sure she'll turn up. She always has in the past."

"Does she go missing often?" asked DJ.

"Oh, sure. Usually after she locks herself out. She starts wandering through the neighborhood, looking for someone to let her in. I keep a spare key to her house just for those times. We all try to keep an eye on her, but sometimes she slips out anyway."

"Have you seen her lately?" I asked.

She wiped a bead of sweat off her brow, thinking. "Let's see. She came by last week, asking if I had a camera."

"A camera? What did she want it for?"

"Taking pictures, she said, of 'something big.' I had some film left on a small camera, so I gave her that." She pulled her garden glove back on and adjusted her straw hat. "Try not to worry about Zola. She'll be back.

Remember the story about the boy who cried wolf? Well, that's Zola. She causes lots of false alarms around here."

I remembered the story. In the end, there really was a wolf.

DJ shaded her eyes and looked across the street. "Let's try Zola's other neighbor."

We crossed over and rang the bell. Mrs. Tucker opened the door and stood there, swaying like a tropical flower in a hot pink shift. She put her finger to her lips and slowly pulled the door closed behind her.

"Ward's resting," she whispered. "He had a bad night."

I gave her a brief recap of how Zola missed our date at the Pizza Pub, and how she hadn't been seen since yesterday.

Mrs. Tucker folded her arms and tapped her chin with her finger. "I'm not certain, but I may know where she went."

"Where?" asked DJ.

"She said something to Ward about going away with her brother for a short trip. I think to the Grand Canyon. He could tell you more about it, but like I said, he's asleep right now."

It didn't make any sense. "Why would she go on a trip?" I asked. "Maybe she meant she was going away to stay with me. She and Mom had it all arranged. How could she forget?"

Mrs. Tucker sighed and threw up her hands. "Zola

does things like that. She can't remember from one day to the next what she has planned. I hope I don't get that way when I'm her age. Just in case, I've got these herb pills called Ginkgo biloba to keep my memory from failing."

"Do they work?" I asked.

She laughed. "I don't know. I keep forgetting to take them."

Chapter 8

"**W**ELL, THAT'S THAT," SAID DJ as we went back to Gran's.

I looked up, puzzled. "What do you mean?"

"Zola's not lost, not wandering around in the desert, and not hanging out at the Indian casino. She's on a trip. She plain forgot all about you."

"Thanks. Being forgotten makes me feel so much better."

But DJ had a point. Zola had forgotten about meeting me once before, the day Mom left. It was like her memory couldn't hold on to anything for very long. So after all our questions, what had we learned?

1) Zola had a history of wandering off.
2) She got mixed up and forgot a lot.
3) She borrowed a camera to use for 'something big.'

The Grand Canyon was big enough. She even had her bag all packed. So when her brother showed up, she probably thought she had packed for that trip. So why was I still worried?

"I don't know, Deej. Something doesn't add up. Some detail is bugging me, but I can't get at it."

DJ opened the front door and let us in. "Try not to think about it so hard. That's what I do when I'm trying to remember something. Then, when your brain is relaxed, BAM! you remember what it was."

We spent the afternoon sorting Gran's stuff. Her bed was piled with dresses, underwear, and shoes, all waiting to be packed. Boxes filled the living room as we added towels, blankets, books, and purses. Stacks of newspapers and tissue littered the floor, ready for wrapping breakable items.

After a while, DJ slumped back on a chair and sighed. "Doing this makes me realize that Gran is really gone. I don't like tearing apart her house and going through her things."

"I know what you mean. It's like we're snooping."

"Too bad your mom couldn't at least keep the place,

furniture and all, and rent it out. Winter visitors would pay lots to rent a nice place like this. Or better yet, you guys could get out of shaky-quaky California and move over here."

I rolled my eyes. "Are you kidding? Move to Geezer City? No way. I'll take the earthquakes."

"Well, think about it. I heard it costs a lot to live in California. You could be here for a lot less. I found a real nice apartment in Tucson for half what I'd pay over there."

What DJ said made some sense. Ever since Dad died, Mom had been worried about the bills. Artists don't exactly have a steady income. That's why I hoped this show in Santa Fe would go well. If she could sell some paintings, maybe she wouldn't have to worry about money all the time.

I picked up a stack of hand-painted plates from the hutch. As I turned, one slipped off my lap and crashed to smithereens.

I bit back a cuss word. "Oooh! That was one of Gran's favorites."

DJ bent down to clean up the pieces. "It's okay. It's not like she's going to come bawl you out."

"If only she could!" I pushed over to the table and set down my load before I dropped anything else. DJ dumped the broken plate in the trash.

"I think you get along pretty well in that chair. A girl

on my team only broke her arm and she made everyone wait on her hand and foot, claiming she was handicapped. We were glad when the team went to finals in Chicago and she had to stay behind."

I let out a huge sigh. "Sometimes I think I can do so much, but then something simple like dropping a dish has to come and remind me."

DJ waved me off. "You're doing great. Coming down here, I wasn't sure what to expect. Last time I saw you, you were still in the hospital. We weren't sure what you'd be able to do. You wouldn't talk to anybody. You wouldn't even try."

"Everything had changed, Deej. My dad had just been killed, my back had been broken. I was scared, too."

"Accidents happen," she said softly. "Don't be so hard on yourself."

I shook my head. "You don't understand. Why did Dad die? Why did I live? I even have nightmares about it. It's like I'm trying to go back and undo what happened. We're driving along, on our way to do some fishing. I see a deer at the side of the road. I'm afraid we'll hit it, so I shout something like 'Watch out!' He swerves, and the Jeep . . . goes over."

I buried my face in my hands. "Sometimes I wish I had died instead. I feel like it was all my fault. I killed my own dad!"

DJ sidled over and gave my shoulders a gentle massage.

"Don't say that! Don't even think it."

I stared at the floor, trying to calm the emotions boiling inside.

She knelt down beside me, tilted my chin up and locked her eyes with mine.

"*Not-your-fault.* Understand? People die. Sometimes it's an accident, sometimes an illness."

I jerked my head away. "At least Gran got to be old before she died."

"Yeah. Gran got lucky."

My eyes wandered across the room, taking in little things that reminded me so much of her. A tin coyote we'd bought once on a visit to Tubac. A crazy quilt she made from old sewing scraps. Her favorite books, especially the one with folktales from Mexico that she used to read to me. "You know, sorting her things makes me feel close to her. I'd bet anything her spirit is lurking around this place, watching us. Don't you feel it?"

"Maybe. Gran was pretty matter-of-fact about death." DJ hunched over a bit and made her voice sound old. "No sad faces, no funeral. Give my sack of bones to the medical center for study. Then go have a party and tell funny stories about me."

That made me smile a little. She sounded just like Gran. I reached out and touched DJ's arm. "Thanks for being here."

I swallowed hard, ready to talk about anything else.

"This job really does take two people. That reminds me, I lost something under one of the twin beds in our room. Can you get it out for me?"

"Sure. Lead the way."

We went to our bedroom and I pointed under the bed. "Down there. It's a roll of tape. Grab that bundle, too."

DJ knelt down and pulled out the tape. Next she hauled out a flat package wrapped in a green, flowered bath towel. She propped it up against the bed. When she drew off the towel, I gasped. The colors were stunning, mostly pale shades of blue. It was a painting of Dad in faded jeans and a blue plaid shirt, working on a stone sculpture. The only touch of strong color was a deep purple handkerchief peeking out from his back pocket. This was *David and Goliath,* the missing painting Mom had been searching for.

"It's supposed to have a silver frame," I said.

DJ crouched down again and peered under the bed. "Nope. Nothing else here." She stared at me. "What's wrong? Not what you expected?"

"No, it's not that." I stared at the painting, feeling glad we had found it but bothered by it, too. "I just don't understand why Gran would have taken the painting out of its frame and then stuck it under the bed."

Later that night, the phone rang. I hurried to answer, relieved to hear Mom's tired voice.

"Hi, Cryssy! How are you doing?"

"Fine. DJ's here."

"You and Zola getting along?"

"Zola never came over, Mom. It looks like she forgot all about me and went on a trip to the Grand Canyon instead."

"Wha-at? How could she do that? Oh Cryssy, I'm sorry. I should have made other arrangements for you."

"I'm fine, Mom. Don't go worrying about me. DJ is here. Everything is fine." I glanced down the hall toward my room. "We found the missing painting."

"You did? That's great!"

"But there's no silver frame with it. Why would Gran have taken it out?"

"I can't imagine. Where did you find the painting?"

"Under a bed in the guest room."

Mom sighed. "I don't know. That's an odd place for Gran to put a painting. With her arthritis, she could barely stoop over."

I hesitated, my mind racing with questions, wondering who else could have put it there. "At least we found it," I said. "We'll save the mystery of how it got there for later."

Chapter 9

THE DREAM WAS BACK. I woke up gasping, as if I'd been running from something I didn't want to see. I lay there staring into the dark, trying to make some sense out of it. Once again I'd been in the white Jeep, zooming along the mountain road. Only this time I was the one driving, not Dad. I remember thinking, *I don't want to go here. I have to turn around before it's too late.* But then the Jeep slowed to a stop. A man with dark hair and paint-spattered clothes stood at the side of the road. I asked if he wanted a lift. He smiled. As he opened the door, a bright blue light flooded into the cab. Then I was out of the Jeep, running away.

I fumbled for my blanket, suddenly feeling cold. I had an uneasy feeling that I wasn't alone. A thin shaft of moonlight filtered through the shuttered window. A faint shape moved in the shadowy corner.

"Is someone there?" I whispered, my voice shaky.

The shape leaned forward into the moonlight. A man dressed in faded jeans and a blue shirt sat with his hands on his knees. I squinted at him, trying to make my eyes focus better. The man shimmered in a thin blue glow. I could see right through to the block wall behind him. A rush of air swirled around the room, lifting my hair and carrying with it a soft voice. *Raniiiiita . . .*

My whole body turned to ice. I knew that voice. I knew that silly nickname, too. Dad used to call me his little frog, or *ranita,* when I was four or five, because I was always hopping on him. I stared at the figure in the chair, especially the touch of gray at his temples, the neat mustache that had always tickled when he kissed me. My eyes wandered to his big sculptor's hands, rough on the outside but gentle in their touch.

I gulped. "Dad? Is that you?"

The breeze in the room died down. He nodded and smiled. The blue halo of light pulsed around him. He crossed his arms in front of his chest and then spread them open, as if sending me a hug.

"Can't you talk to me?"

He held his fingers about an inch apart in a "little bit"

sign. I glanced over at the painting, leaning against the wall. "You led me to the painting of you, didn't you?"

The blue light around him pulsed.

"Have you been here all along?"

The ghost nodded.

"Did Gran see you?"

He nodded again, but as he did, he shimmered and changed. Now he was a young boy, the boy Gran had raised.

I tried to remember what I'd heard about ghosts. Didn't they hang around when they couldn't rest? Was Dad a restless spirit?

"Why are you here? What's bothering you?"

The boy hung his head. When he looked up, he was older again. He shook his head, his eyes sad. He pointed to my wheelchair.

"The accident? It was all my fault! I made you look away from the road. I've been wanting to tell you how sorry I was, but—"

He jumped up. He waved his arms and shook his head no. Then he pointed to his chest.

"What are you trying to say?"

He held out his hand toward my legs as the air in the room swirled around me again. "I'm sorry!" he whispered.

I wanted to rush into his arms and say it was all right. "Don't be upset, Dad. Look at me. I'm getting along fine."

He nodded and then folded his hands, as if begging

something from me. The blue light pulsed brighter than ever, and the air whooshed by me, carrying with it the words, "Be careful, *Ranita!*"

With that, the blue glow faded to black and Dad was gone. I sat there holding my breath, staring at the empty chair until it, too, melted into inky puddles of darkness.

Chapter 10

WHEN I WOKE IN THE MORNING, my first thought was, *What a crazy dream!* But had it been only a dream? It seemed so real, and I was sure I hadn't been asleep. Little details came back to me, like the way the wind had sifted through my hair and the soft tremble in Dad's voice. Just thinking about it gave me goosebumps again. As I got dressed I considered talking to DJ about it, but I was afraid she'd just laugh at me. Besides, I wasn't sure I wanted to share my experience. Real or not, Dad's visit was mine, all mine.

After breakfast Mom called again, needing reassurance

that we were okay. I was not going to tell her about my ghostly "visit" from Dad. That would *really* worry her.

"So, how's the show going?" I asked. "Sold any paintings?"

"Yes! One sold right away—that one of the lighthouse that you liked. Then an art critic came by. He wrote a nice piece in the paper . . ."

As she rambled on, full of excitement about the show, I glanced out the window toward Zola's house. A man ducked out of her front door, hugging a brown shopping bag to his chest. He had a wide-brimmed straw hat on, so I couldn't see his face.

". . . and today I already got offers on two more. How about that?"

Her question whizzed right by me. The man hopped in a golf cart and chugged down the street.

"Cryssy?" Mom's voice brought me back.

"That's great news! Maybe you'll see him—I mean, sell them."

"I hope so. Take care now. Call me if there's any news about Zola."

I put down the phone and hustled out the front door. By then, the man in the golf cart was nowhere to be seen. I went back inside just as DJ came down the hall, brushing her hair.

"Some guy just came out of Zola's place," I told her.

"Really? Who?"

"I don't know. I was on the phone with Mom when I saw him. I think he's stolen something."

"Let's go see."

We hurried across the street, but now Zola's door was locked. The man must have set the lock when he shut the door. Such a careful, thoughtful thief.

"Rats! How will we get in?"

DJ grinned. "Pick the lock?"

"No, wait. Didn't the neighbor hacking at her tree say she had a key to Zola's house? Run over there and see if she's home."

In a few minutes DJ was back, a brass house key dangling from her finger. "We're in business, *chica*."

As we eased into the living room, things looked different. A chair sat straighter. The towels had been picked up. It almost looked normal. Then I noticed the sofa. Zola's pink dress was folded neatly beside her overnight case. But something was missing.

"Her purse is gone!" I cried.

"You're right. Stay here. I'm going to take a quick look-see through the rest of the place." DJ disappeared down the hall.

"I'll check outside," I called after her. My face and arms felt prickly as I inched across the room. I scanned everything as I went, looking for anything else missing. Outside, the patio looked cozy and quiet. Two cactus-filled clay bowls nestled in one corner. A wrought iron table and one chair were in the other corner. The second wrought iron chair was blocking my way, and I had to maneuver around it. A hummingbird buzzed over my head, making me look up. He poked his long beak into a red feeder suspended from the overhang. A lopsided basket of plastic flowers hung nearby, their once–bright red color now faded to pink from the sun.

DJ came out, her hands on her hips. "*Nada*. Anything out here?"

"You're tall, Deej. What can you see over the walls?"

She peered over the left wall. "Tuckers' patio. Not much there." She moved to the back wall. "Swimming pool." Then the other neighboring wall. "A fake putting green, golf balls, patio furniture, and a small table."

I looked back to the chair and noticed that it was directly under the basket of flowers. Why was it there, when the table was across the patio? Had Zola had used it to put something in the basket for some reason?

"Check that hanging basket. See if there's anything in it besides those dumb flowers."

She climbed onto the chair and fumbled in the basket. Her eyes widened as she pulled out a roll of film.

"Looky here! How did you know?"

I shrugged. "That chair. It didn't look like it belonged there, right in front of the patio door."

DJ tossed the roll of film around in her hand. "Think Zola stashed it there?"

"Probably."

"But why?"

I drummed my fingers on my armrests, trying to imagine what would make Zola want to stash a roll of film. It didn't seem like something she would do because she was forgetful. If she was just confused, she might have put it in the refrigerator or the oven. No, this had the feel of a deliberate act, an attempt to hide it from someone. Maybe that someone was the man I saw sneaking out of her house.

"Let's call the cops and report the prowler," I said. "Then we'll drop that film off at the drugstore to be developed."

One benefit of a small town is that the cops come right away when you call them. Maybe they just didn't have enough juicy crime to keep them busy. The officer who met us at the door was short and compact, with thick black hair swept back from his face. Under a shiny badge, his name tag read "Mike Lawrence."

"Thanks for coming so fast," DJ said, opening the door wide so I could go out.

He took out his pad and pen. "You reported a prowler?"

"Yes, coming out of our neighbor's house over there." I pointed across to Zola's place. "We're worried about her, too. Her name is Zola Waselewski, and she's been gone since Sunday."

"Are you a relative?"

I gave a brief explanation of how we knew Zola and told him that she was a friend of the family who was supposed to be staying with me. And I explained about finding her house empty.

The officer frowned at us like we were the criminals, not the ones who had called him. "Why were you in her house?" he asked.

I took a deep breath. "The man I saw come out of there had a brown paper bag in his arms. We checked to see if anything was missing, and there is. Zola's purse is gone."

"Can you describe the man? Old, young, short, fat?"

"He was tall. Definitely an adult, but I couldn't tell how old. His face was hidden by his big straw hat. He left in a white golf cart, if that helps."

The officer scribbled more notes in his book, flipped it shut, and tapped the cover with his pen. He squinted at us, looking down his nose. "You girls stay out of that house from now on. I'm going to have a look around. You could have run into real trouble, you know."

"We had to check!" I snapped back. His attitude was not making me a fan of the police.

He put his hands on his hips and glared at me. "Prowlers don't like being surprised. Let the police handle things from now on. I'll have a talk with the other neighbors, to see if they saw anyone suspicious." He fished a card out of his shirt pocket and handed it to DJ. "If anything else happens, call 911 or this number at the station."

We stayed by the front window to watch what he did. Officer Lawrence walked around the outside of Zola's place, checking the door to make sure it was locked. Then he went to Mr. Andrews's house. A few minutes later, he crossed over to the Tuckers' place.

"Maybe we should have told him about the film," said DJ.

"Uh-uh. Not until we see what's on it."

I looked out the front window again. He'd finished talking with the Tuckers and was headed back our way. We met him at the door again.

The officer jerked his thumb across the street. "The neighbors say Mrs. Waselewski told them she was going with her brother to the Grand Canyon. So apparently she's not missing after all."

I shook my head. "But Zola never said anything about her brother coming or about going away. She promised my mom she'd stay with me."

"And what about her purse being stolen?" asked DJ. "We did see a prowler come out of her house."

The cop tucked his notepad into his pocket. "I made a note of that, and we'll keep an eye on the place. I'm sure Mrs. Waselewski appreciates your watching her house for her, but don't you two start playing junior detectives. If she's simply away on a trip, she'll be back soon."

I shut the door with a huff. "He didn't believe us at all!" I told DJ. "He thinks we're just a couple of ditsy girls with nothing else to do. Come on, Deej. Let's drop that film off."

Chapter 11

THE DRUGSTORE OFFERED ONLY ONE-DAY SERVICE, but at least we beat the pick-up time for the film. I hoped we'd find out the next day why Zola had stashed it in that flower basket. Outside, we followed the aroma of fresh-baked cinnamon rolls into a small bakery. We bought a couple of gooey rolls and sat outdoors at a small table.

DJ shoved the extra chair aside so I could wheel close in. "I bet when we get those photos back, there won't be anything weird about them," she said.

I set the brakes and thought a moment. "Then why would Zola hide that film?"

DJ took a big bite of her cinnamon roll. "Because she's mixed up," she mumbled, her mouth full. "No one else seems to think that her being gone—at least for a while—is all that unusual."

"What about the guy I saw coming out of her house?"

She shrugged. "Zola could have asked him to check her place while she was gone. He did make sure the door was locked when he left."

I picked at the frosting on my roll. "You think I'm overreacting?"

"Maybe. While we're sitting here worrying, she's probably up in the cool high country having a great time."

I took a deep breath and looked out across the parking lot. Fat gray doves waddled around in the shade, trying to stay cool. One sipped water from a small puddle that had been made by the sprinkler. For Zola's sake, I hoped DJ was right.

As we cruised down Manzanita Avenue, I still kept my eyes open for a little old lady wandering down the street. When we passed a small strip mall, a familiar face caught my eye.

I grabbed DJ's arm. "Slow down a minute."

"Why? What happened?"

"I just saw Matt going into that pawn shop."

"So?"

"Why would he go to a pawn shop? It's not exactly a kid hangout."

She slowed the car, made a U-turn, and pulled into the parking lot. The pawn shop sat next to a used clothing store. Bars covered the windows, and bright streamers—the kind used car dealers have—flapped from the roof.

DJ grinned. "I've never been in a pawn shop. Maybe it's time to find out what they're like. You know, in case I lose my scholarship."

We had to ring a buzzer by the front door just to get admitted. Inside, it wasn't anything like a regular store like Wal-Mart or Target. Long glass cases lined the walls, jammed with guns, knives, jewelry, and cameras. Stacked behind the counters were televisions, VCRs, computers, and small appliances. It had the jumbled look of a garage sale times ten.

The scariest thing was seeing the clerk wearing a gun. He was talking to Matt when we came in, then went in the back for a moment. From the ceiling, security cameras monitored our every move. Matt moved to a rack of bicycles and checked out a sporty mountain bike.

I edged up behind him. "Hey, stranger. Fancy meeting you here."

He turned, surprised. "Same to you." He pulled the bike out and looked it over, rolling it back and forth.

"Cool, huh? I need some kind of wheels while Dad is at his office. What are you guys up to?"

I shrugged. "Nothing much."

Matt went back to fiddling with the bike, trying out the hand brakes and checking the tread on the tires.

DJ suddenly grabbed my chair and turned me around. "Hey, Crystal, look up there!" She pointed to something hanging on the wall above the jewelry counter. "Is that the silver frame you were looking for?"

I followed her gaze to a silver frame, my hopes soaring. But it was just an ordinary silver painted frame, not the fancy one Gran had.

"Nope, not it. Gran's was real silver."

The clerk was watching us all the time, probably trying to decide if we were real customers or just shoplifters. He ambled over. "Help you kids with something?"

"Have you ever taken in a silver picture frame? About so big." I held up my hands to show him. "It had pieces of turquoise inlay in it."

"Nope. Can't say that I have." The entry bell sounded, and he buzzed in a new customer.

As Matt replaced the bike, he had a look of mischief in his eyes. "I can get the bike later. How about going for a drive? We can grab some Cokes and hamburgers at McDonald's. Then I'll show you my ranch."

"You have your own ranch?" asked DJ.

He flashed a devilish smile. "Haven't you heard? I'm a big shot landowner now."

My heart did a flip, and I wondered if he had any idea how cute he was. I turned to DJ, pointed my nose to the sky, and waved my hand at her. "Oh, chauffeur? Please bring Mr. Big Shot's limo around."

DJ bowed deeply. "Yes, Madam. Im-meed-jut-ly!"

Chapter 12

As we headed south toward Nogales, DJ brought Matt up to date about Zola, about calling in the cops, and the Tuckers saying Zola told had gone to the Grand Canyon. Hearing her recap, I felt there was still a piece of the puzzle hiding in my brain. The more I tried to get at it, the better it hid.

I stared out the window, wondering how long a person could survive in the desert. If Zola was lost and not off on a trip, she wouldn't stand a chance out there. The heat shimmered off the rocks and the sand. At least it wasn't like the barren sand dunes we had driven by near Yuma, where all those off-road racers went tearing around. The desert here had prickly pear and cholla cactus, scrub brush, and scraggly mesquite trees.

DJ slowed as two skinny coyotes darted across the road. She glanced in the rear-view mirror and winced. "Yikes! That van almost hit us! Back off, creep!" She watched the mirror for a few moments, then relaxed. "That's better. He's staying back now."

About twenty miles south of Copper Valley, Matt told DJ to take the Mariposa Canyon exit. The tailgating van zoomed on down the highway. The exit ramp brought us onto a dirt road. It followed a rocky ridge overlooking the valley below.

After a mile or so, Matt said, "Pull over by that flat outcrop. There's a great view from up there."

DJ parked the car, and she and Matt hopped out. I stayed put. There was no way I could maneuver my wheelchair on this rocky, uneven ground.

"You guys go on ahead. I'll just wait here."

"Nothing doing," said Matt, opening my door. "You grab one end, DJ, I'll take the other."

DJ shoved him aside. "Don't be smart, Mr. Big Shot." She bent over and slid her arms under my thighs. "Now wrap your arms around my neck. I'll carry you over there."

"Are you sure?"

"Sure I'm sure."

I did as I was told, choking back the embarrassment of being carried like a big baby. Matt must have sensed how I felt. He turned away, keeping his eyes on the view instead of on me.

"Light as a feather," said DJ. In moments she had settled me on top of the rocks, where I could see everything. A range of jagged mountains rose from the valley floor. Just below the ridge, a small stream coursed its way through a grove of cottonwood trees. Overhead, a hawk floated silently on an updraft of air. This was much better than sitting in the car.

"Thanks, Deej. What a great view!" A childhood memory flashed in my mind, making me chuckle.

"What's so funny?" asked DJ.

"I was remembering that when I was little, I used to worry that I'd go blind someday. We had this kid in my second-grade class who was blind, and I wondered what it would be like. So I used to practice feeling my way around our house with my eyes shut, just in case. I guess I should have practiced getting around with no legs instead."

DJ looked at me like I was out of my mind. "You're a very strange person, you know?"

"Well, anyway, I'm just happy I'm not blind. I'd be missing this great view!"

Matt stepped up on the rock, spread his arms out, and hollered, "I am the master of all you survey!"

"Yeah, right. You own all this," huffed DJ, turning her cap so the visor was in front, where it shaded her eyes.

"Yep. At least for a while, Dad says. See that flat mountain to the south? That's how close we are to Mexico. From here to that bend in the river down there is my land. It's a little complicated. Dad wanted to buy this chunk of land, but he had to be kind of sneaky about it."

"So he bought it in your name? Is that legal?" I asked.

"Yeah, I guess so. It's really in a trust for me, but under my name and all."

"What's he going to do with the land. Develop it?" asked DJ.

"Maybe. This area is a bird sanctuary. I think Dad's plan has something to do with keeping lots of open space. It's real hush-hush right now. He wants to keep it a secret for a few more days. Then something big is supposed to happen."

Secret? And there were those words again—something big. Could Zola have known about this plan and caused trouble? She sure had reasons to get back at Horrible Horace. He'd been one of those who had gotten her driver's license taken away, and he wanted her moved to a nursing home.

"Do you think Zola knew about this?" I asked.

Matt shrugged and tossed a rock into the sagebrush below. "Maybe." Then he turned and wrinkled his nose at me. "Hey, you think my old man offed Zola, don't you? Now that's funny!"

"I'm just thinking out loud, trying out ideas."

Matt sat down on the flat rock, crossed his legs, and

stared up at the sky. "Well, do me one favor, okay? Scratch my old man off your idea list. He may be a jerk in lots of ways, but he's not the kind to hurt anyone on purpose. He's full of hot air—most of the time."

DJ tossed another rock into the canyon. "Is it true he had the swimming pool closed because there wasn't a lifeguard?"

Matt looked puzzled. "That's not why it's closed. Someone dumped too much chlorine in. You swim in that and your skin gets real itchy and your eyes burn. It takes a week or so to neutralize the water."

"Well I hope they get it finished soon. I'm melting here, and a nice dip in the pool would sure feel good," said DJ.

Nobody said anything for a while. We munched our hamburgers and listened to the wind rustling through the canyon. All these bits of information were swirling around in my brain, too. Matt wouldn't even consider the idea that his dad might be involved. I guessed it was natural to defend your own dad. Knots of envy tightened my stomach. At least Matt had a real live dad to stick up for. All I had was a ghost, or a dream. I wasn't sure what I had.

So many questions nagged at me. If only Dad were here right now to help us hash them out. For example, who would consider Zola a threat? Was an old lady a reliable witness to anything? Everyone said she got confused and acted strangely. If I were a cop, I sure wouldn't believe her.

We dropped Matt off at the golf club to meet his dad, then headed home. A minute after we got in, the doorbell rang. Ward Tucker was standing there, grinning from ear to ear, with a wrapped package under his arm. Today he was dressed in overalls and looked more like a hard-working elf than Santa.

"Hey there! Glad you're home. Didn't want to just leave this by the door. I meant to return it to your grandmother weeks ago. Sorry about the delay." He placed the package on my lap.

"What is it?"

"Take a look. Came out real nice."

It felt like a painting. Gently, I tore off the tape and let the brown wrapping paper fall to the floor. I smiled as I ran my fingers across a smooth silver frame, stopping to touch the turquoise chunks embedded at the corners. This was the frame that belonged to the *David and Goliath* painting of Dad. Only now it held a different painting, one of the desert at sunset.

"Come here, Deej. Look at this!"

She scooted over. "Cool."

Mr. Tucker grasped the straps of his overalls, looking very proud of himself. "It's by a local artist. We picked it up at one of our swap meets. Before she got sick, your grandmother brought this frame over for repair. It was cracked." He pointed a chubby finger along the base. "Right there in front. You can't tell now. Metalwork's a hobby of mine."

"It looks perfect," I said.

"But isn't the painting yours?" asked DJ.

"Nope. Emilia saw it when she brought the frame over. Bought it right on the spot and asked us to use her frame. Guess that makes it part of her estate now."

I reached around to my backpack, fumbling for my wallet. "Thanks for bringing it over. What do we owe you for the repairs?"

He waved me off, turning to head home. "Not a thing. All paid for in advance."

"A question before you leave," said DJ. "When Zola told you she was going to the Grand Canyon, did she mention Crystal ? Zola was supposed to be staying here this week."

He tugged at his bushy white mustache, glancing nervously over at Zola's house. "Nope. Not a word. She just asked me to keep an eye on her place." He stepped out into the street, adding, "Like I told you before, she's real forgetful. Doesn't do you two any good, though, does it?"

"We're okay," I said. "Thanks for bringing this over."

After he left, I hurried down to my room to get the painting of Dad. It was the one that belonged in this frame—not that crummy sunset. I couldn't imagine Gran buying something that looked like a paint-by-numbers job. She knew good art. And Mom's painting of Dad was very good art.

Chapter 13

"DO YOU BELIEVE IN GHOSTS?" I asked DJ the next morning. After mulling it over, I had decided to take a chance and ask her. We were eating breakfast on Gran's patio.

She leaned her elbows on the table, thinking for a moment. "I took a psych class at the U last fall. We talked about paranormal stuff. We even went on a field trip to Bisbee for a tour of the Copper Queen Hotel. It's famous for having ghosts."

"So is that a yes or a no?"

"I don't know. Before I said yes, I'd like to see one."

"What if I've seen one?"

"You have? Where?"

I pointed toward the house. "Here. In my room."

That made her sit up. "Was it Gran?"

"No, it was my dad."

She let out a whistle. "You're creeping me out here, *chica*. Why would his ghost be in Gran's house?"

I sighed and looked up at Gran's wind chimes. They tinkled gently in the morning breeze. "I think he's here because I'm here. He seemed to be saying he felt guilty about the accident."

Her eyes grew wide. "He talked to you?"

"Sort of. It was weird, really weird."

"What does this ghost look like?"

"It looks like him, only see-through. Sometimes he's just a blue glow with no shape, just a . . . presence. It's hard to explain."

She looked at me like I'd gone mental. She raised her hands over her head and wiggled her fingers in the air. "Ooooooh! This I gotta see. Let me know the next time he floats by."

I stared at my plate as hot waves of anger rolled up my neck. Tears welled up in my eyes and my mouth clamped shut. DJ didn't understand at all. From now on, I'd keep my ghost to myself.

DJ stood, collected her dishes and started to head back inside. "By the way, I've got to go up to the university today. Will it be okay to leave you alone for a while?"

I glared at her, still mad about her reaction. "Of course. I'm not a baby, you know."

She hesitated. "I might be gone most of the day. I've got to see my advisor about fall classes, and there's a training meeting with the team."

"Fine. I'll pack up some more of Gran's stuff."

"Are you sure you'll be all right?"

"*Yessss,*" I hissed. "Don't be such a mother hen."

After she left, I was glad to be alone for a while. I was still ticked off about her attitude and mad at myself for sharing my secret with her. Trying to forget about it, I spent some time sorting old videos and stacking the keepers in a box by the television. Mostly they were the home videos we'd made for Gran. The other ones were musicals and nature subjects, perfect for a garage sale. I sighed as I looked them over. Why did people have to die?

Gran had told me once that she believed in spirits, in the "presence" of someone who had died. After Granddad died, she said he was still near her, watching over her and keeping her company. Wishful thinking, I used to think. Now I understood. But if my "ghost" came again, I was definitely not telling DJ.

About mid-morning, Anna Norberg from next door came over. She moved some newspapers off a dining chair and sat so we were eye to eye. I appreciated that, because then I didn't have to look up at her all the time.

"Want some iced tea, Ms. Norberg?"

"No, thanks. And call me Anna, please. I was just wondering if you'd heard from Zola."

I shook my head. "We called the police after we saw someone come out of Zola's house."

She leaned forward, her brows raised. "Really? Could it have been a maintenance man? They were there earlier, but of course no one was home."

"No, it was some guy carrying a paper sack. Tell me, what kind of truck did the maintenance guys have?"

"One of those little tan pickups. It had the word 'maintenance' on one side. Why do you ask?"

"Just curious." I felt my shoulders tense. Now I was sure the panel truck I saw should not have been at Zola's.

"What did the policeman say?" Anna asked.

"Mostly he told us to mind our own business. The Tuckers claim Zola told them she went to the Grand Canyon with her brother from Chicago."

Anna sat back, her forehead wrinkled. "I don't know about that. She told me once that her brother was quite infirm. I got the impression he never went anywhere."

This was not sounding good. Not good at all.

"I came over because I remembered something Zola said about needing that camera. She talked about thieves in the neighborhood." Anna paused and mimicked Zola's accent.

"'They think I not zee, but I do zee!' She was as happy as a kid with a new toy. She left muttering, 'I get zem, you vill zee!' Sometimes you almost need an interpreter to understand her."

I muffled a laugh. It really wasn't funny, but I couldn't help it.

"I'll tell you one thing she's got right," Anna said.

"What's that?"

"Somebody has been helping themselves to things around here. I had to give Zola that cheap little camera because my good one was stolen, along with a lot of expensive photo equipment." Anna closed her eyes and sighed. "This used to be such a quiet town. Ward Tucker claims they're missing a set of silver, too. But with all the stuff they have over there, I don't know how he could tell whether something was missing or just buried."

I sat for a moment, mulling over this new information. What did Zola mean about getting someone? Did they get her instead?

Anna stood up. "Have you checked the social center? Today was Zola's dance class. She never misses. I think she has a boyfriend!"

A boyfriend? I felt a glimmer of hope. Maybe he would know something about Zola. But how was I going to get to the center? With DJ gone, I had no transportation. "Could you give me a lift to the center? My cousin's gone up to Tucson, and I'm stuck."

"Sure," Anna said. "Come over in ten minutes and we'll be off."

Chapter 14

COPPER VALLEY BOASTED THAT IT HAD SEVEN social centers to serve the residents. Each offered a bunch of activities ranging from computers and woodworking to photography, ceramics, dancing, and more. I remembered Gran saying how nice it was to have so many activities to choose from. She was never bored.

Anna pulled her red Volvo into the parking lot of the West Hills Center. Several pale pink buildings spread out from a central courtyard. Water splashed in a Spanish-style fountain in the middle, surrounded by sprays of purple bougainvillea and other wispy desert plants with bright orange and yellow flowers.

"Want me to pick you up?" she asked, helping me into my chair.

"No. I'll find a way back. Thanks!"

"Call if you can't. I'm in the book."

For once, I was glad to be in a town designed for old folks. Everything was wheelchair accessible. I headed over to what looked like the main building. A bulletin board on the outside was cluttered with announcements of classes and visiting artists, descriptions of lost cats, and business cards.

At the information desk inside, a lady with poofy blonde hair sat playing solitaire on her computer. When I asked about a dance class, she quickly ended the game and pointed across the lobby.

"In there. Just follow the music."

The double doors opened into a huge multipurpose room. Folding chairs lined the walls or were stacked on a cart, leaving the floor open. A clogging class was in full swing, and fiddle music filled the air. About ten couples practiced steps, following the instructor. I scanned the room for a familiar face. No Zola. At the break, a lanky man wearing cowboy boots, a red checkered western shirt, and a neckerchief came over. I tried not to stare at his hair, which looked like it had been dyed with orange soda.

"Yer Zola's new friend, ain't ya," he said, hooking his thumbs in his pockets.

"How do you know?"

"Zola told me all about ya," he said, holding out his hand. "I'm Milton. Where is she, anyhoo? I called over at her place, but she wasn't there."

I counted the possible ideas on my fingers. "One neighbor thinks she just wandered off again. Another says she went on a trip. I think something worse happened."

Milton ran his hand through his wild hair. "That don't sound good. She wouldn't go away and not tell me."

"When did you talk to her last?"

He rubbed his chin, thinking. "Must've been Saturday afternoon. I rang her up for a chat, but she cut it short. Something about takin' pitchers."

"Pictures of what?"

"She didn't say. I've been askin' all her friends, but no one has seen her." A new song filled the room, and the dancers started to choose partners. He turned to leave. "Hey, that's my cue. You gotta find her. She never misses a class."

I nodded, then smiled, imagining Zola out there dancing. She'd really been looking forward to this class. Milton's comment about her taking pictures matched what Anna had said. But why would taking pictures get her lost? I headed back to the front lobby and outside to the fountain.

Shading my eyes from the bright sunlight, I wished I'd brought my sunglasses. There were more classrooms across the patio. Signs on the doors said "Lapidary," "Woodworking," and "Ceramics." This must be where Matt came for his lapidary class. Slowly, I wheeled by each classroom. They were empty now, the lessons over, and the lights were dimmed. As I turned down the sidewalk, I thought someone called out my name in a harsh whisper.

Crystal . . . over here.

Without thinking, I followed the raspy sound into the ceramics room. The door stood open, the room half lit. Four long work tables filled the room, wiped clean for the day. Unfinished clay projects lined the shelves in the back of the room. It didn't look like anyone was there. I turned to leave.

You are looking for me?

I strained to listen. Was that Zola's voice I'd heard? My pulse quickened. The voice seemed to come from a lighted room in the back. I zigzagged my way around the worktables toward the sound.

"Zola? Is that you?" I asked. Pushing the door open wider, I eased into a crowded storeroom. Three silvery kilns took up most of the area, emitting a steady warmth like giant round ovens. Along the walls, painted but unglazed rabbits, clowns, and vases waited to be finished and fired.

"Anyone here?" I asked.

As if in answer, the light went out and the door banged

shut behind me. I backed up, trying to turn around in the tight space. My chair knocked against the shelving. Clay figures crashed to the floor. I reached behind me, fumbling frantically for the doorknob. It wasn't locked, but I couldn't push the door open, either. Something was blocking it. Panic prickled inside me as I felt the temperature in the room begin to rise. I strained to focus in the near-total darkness. All I could make out were the eerie red numbers ticking off the baking time on the kilns. They were like little eyes, watching me, waiting for me.

"Hey! Let me out of here!" I shouted.

My voice slammed back at me. I banged on the door and waited. No one came. So much for thinking I could handle things on my own. My scalp grew damp, and sweat trickled down my neck. Now what? I wondered if anyone ever came to check on the kilns. How was I going to get out of here?

I held my breath, listening. A drop of sweat plunked from my eyebrow into my eye. *Calm down, calm down,* I told myself, rubbing away the drop. *Take a deep breath. Relax.* The earthy smell of baking clay filled my nose. An image of Gran floated in my memory, of her scolding me for doing something stupid. "*Antes que te cases, mira lo que haces,*" she'd warn me when I was about to get myself into trouble. It meant something along the lines of "Look before you leap."

Trapped in the darkness, old fears swarmed over me

like pesky beetles—fears from the other time I was trapped, after the accident. *Why doesn't someone come? Hasn't anyone seen the wreck? Why is Dad so still? Why can't I feel my legs? Maybe they're trapped under something. Dad? Dad? Oh, Daddy . . . please don't die!*

I closed my eyes and concentrated on the raspy voice that lured me in here. Who knew my name, or that I'd even be here? Had I really heard a voice? Yes, I was sure of it. But was it Zola's voice or someone trying to sound like her? The heat was making me groggy, and I wondered how long I'd been stuck in here. Ten minutes? Twenty minutes? More?

My only hope was to get that door open, at least wide enough to let in some fresh air, and so I could call out. There wasn't enough room to turn around, so I shoved my chair backwards, banging against the door. I tried again, pushing harder on my wheels. The door moved a tiny bit, letting in a welcome shaft of light. Now I could see better.

I spotted a broom in the corner, propped against the wall. I reached out and grabbed it. Sticking the handle in the crack of the door, I pried it back and forth. Each movement opened the door a little wider. I could hear something scraping against the floor—probably a chair or table propped against the door to keep it from opening. Finally, the door opened enough to let me turn my chair a little. I reached out and shoved hard. A worktable groaned with movement, and the door opened wide.

I pushed myself across the floor and onto the sun-drenched patio, gulping the fresh air. Brightness dazzled my eyes, forcing them closed for a moment.

When my heart finally stopped jumping up and down like a grasshopper and my breathing was back to normal, questions screamed at me. Who shut me in there, and why? An ugly thought sent a chill through me. Someone definitely wasn't happy with my nosing around, and that could mean only one thing. Zola wasn't just lost or away on some trip. She'd been kidnapped. And whoever did it was trying to stop me from finding her.

I needed answers, but I couldn't get them here. I gave my wheels an angry shove and headed back to the main hall and the woman at the information desk.

"Where can I get a bus?"

"Bus? 'Fraid not," the woman replied. "There aren't any buses in Copper Valley. I can call you a cab."

Great, just great. How can there be no buses in this stupid town? The few dollars I had in my backpack probably weren't enough for a cab ride. Now what? Call Anna Norberg to come back for me?

As if in answer to a prayer, I spotted Matt and his dad across the patio. Today they were dressed in tennis whites and carrying racquets.

"Mr. Andrews! Matt! Wait up!"

Mr. Andrews turned. This time he recognized me.

"Hey, little lady. What are you doing here? Slumming with the old folks?"

"I'm looking for your neighbor, Zola."

"She's still not home?" he asked.

"No. I thought she might be here at her dance class."

Matt tilted his head, staring at me. "Are you okay? Your face is all red."

I was too upset to explain how I got shut in the ceramics room. "It's just the sun. I'm not used to this heat. Are you two on your way home? I could use a lift."

"Sure. We were just leaving," said Mr. Andrews. "I need to make one stop at my office first. On our way there, you can fill us in on your search. Maybe we can help."

Feeling grateful for the ride, I agreed. It would give me a chance to talk to Matt again. But why was Mr. Andrews so concerned about Zola now? He hadn't seemed very interested in looking for her yesterday. Maybe he just wanted to find out what I was up to.

Chapter 15

When Mr. Andrews dropped me off, DJ sprinted out to meet me, her face a mix of anger and relief.

"*¡Ay bendito!* Thank God you're okay!"

"Why? What's happened?" I asked.

"Come see for yourself." DJ shoved the door open wide, letting me inside.

The place was a total mess, and not just the packing mess we'd made. The house had been ransacked. Sofa cushions leaned on each other like dominoes. Gran's tiny knickknacks lay scattered on the floor. In the kitchen, drawers hung at awkward angles, and a few had been dumped out. Every cupboard was wide open. Some of the boxes we'd so carefully packed and sealed were ripped open. A bag of groceries leaned against the entry wall.

I felt the color drain from my face. "Oh, my God! Were we robbed?"

DJ's hand flew to her chest. "I just got home. When I saw this mess and then couldn't find you, my heart about stopped. Another ten seconds and I would have called the cops. Where were you, anyway?"

"I was over at the social center, looking for Zola and asking questions. I had a little trouble, though. Someone shut me in a sweltering kiln room."

DJ's mouth dropped open. "What?"

"I'm all right. It took me a while, but I forced the door open and got out. Matt and his dad brought me home."

"Good grief!" She picked up the bag of groceries and trudged into the kitchen. "Actually, it's a good thing you weren't here when all this happened."

As I scanned the "scene of the crime," a thought hit me like a two-by-four. "I bet whoever did this knew I wouldn't be here. Someone obviously doesn't like that we've been asking about Zola. Whoever trapped me in that kiln room knew you were gone, too. A perfect time to come ransack this place."

"Good point. Scary, but good," DJ said. She started scooping up the silverware and utensils scattered on the floor, then stopped. "Before this happened, I thought you were going overboard with your suspicions. But now I've changed my mind. Now we call 911."

Ten minutes later, good old Officer Lawrence was back, this time with an evidence technician who started dusting for fingerprints. We were taken more seriously this time.

The cop made a pass through every room, then came back to the living room. "Anything missing?" he asked.

DJ shrugged as she scanned the front room. "It's hard to tell. Part of this mess is our own doing. We're packing up our grandmother's stuff. But we did not toss sofa cushions to the floor or dump out drawers or pull the mattresses off the beds."

He handed DJ a form to fill out. "You can bring this down to the station after you've checked what's missing. It looks to me like someone was searching the place. Any drugs or weapons here?"

I shook my head. "No way. Gran wouldn't touch a gun. The only drugs were her medications, and we flushed those soon after she died."

"Well, if nothing's missing, maybe the person who did this got nothing. I see your TV and VCR are still here. That's good."

Frankly, I didn't see anything good about it. Someone had broken into the house. I wondered if I'd feel safe here anymore.

After the cops left, we started cleaning up. I did what I could to shove drawers closed. "I'm worried that Zola's really in trouble," I told DJ. "Someone has either hurt her, locked her away, or . . . oh God. What if she's dead?"

"Don't scare me like that. What kind of threat could an old lady be?"

"You don't have to be young and spry to see things you shouldn't."

DJ reached into her tote bag. "You know, I'm wondering if our burglar was looking for this." She held up a yellow-and-white envelope. "On my way here, I stopped at the drugstore and picked up Zola's pictures."

"Excellent!" I said, excited again. "Let's see what we have."

It had been a 24-exposure roll, but not all of them came out. We spread the photos out on the kitchen table, separating them. Ten showed some family at Christmas—kids opening presents, mugging for the camera, that sort of thing. But the last four photos were different.

"There's Anna Norberg in her patio," I said.

"Not a very good shot. She put her hands up like she didn't want her picture taken."

The next one showed part of a different patio. A youngish man looked like he was cleaning golf clubs, or maybe repairing them. Three other golf bags were piled beside him. Boxes were stacked in the background, possibly other jobs needing work.

"Whose patio is that?" asked DJ.

"Beats me. All these patios look alike." I picked up another photo. It showed Mr. Andrews bending over to sort some papers that lay open on a table. I laughed. "He'd sure be ticked if he knew Zola took a picture of his butt."

The last photo was another patio, empty, except for a lawn chair with tattered webbing in the seat.

"It's the Tuckers' patio," said DJ. "I remember seeing that ratty chair when I looked over the wall."

"This is useless," I said, leaning back in my chair. "I was hoping we'd find something suspicious." I looked at the last photo again. "There's someone by the sliding glass door. It's probably one of the Tuckers."

DJ peered closer at it. "Hmm. That's real suspicious, all right. Standing in your own house, looking out to your own patio."

I put the photos down. "I'm confused. Why take pictures of patios? I hoped she'd have pictures of burglars breaking into houses or something. This doesn't look like anything that would get her in trouble."

We spread out the photos and ran through them again.

"Maybe the clue is what *isn't* in the photos," suggested DJ.

I sighed. "Great. How are we supposed to figure that out?" I returned the photos to their envelope and slipped the package into my backpack. Maybe later something about them would make sense.

DJ started unpacking cheese, avocado, and tortillas from the grocery bag. "All this high intrigue is making me hungry. Want some quesadillas?"

"Yeah. I'll grate the cheese." I reached for a cutting board and grater and balanced them on my lap.

"So tell me what happened today," DJ said, putting a big skillet on the stove. "Don't leave anything out."

"After Anna Norberg dropped me at the social center, I started asking around for Zola. I met her dance partner, by the way. He seemed really worried about her. He's been looking for her, too."

"How did you end up trapped?"

I hiked my shoulders. "I was just checking the place out. Then I heard someone call my name. "

"Man's voice or woman's voice?"

"I couldn't tell. It was a raspy whisper. It almost sounded like Zola's voice. Next thing I know, wham! I'm stuck in that hot, dark room."

DJ cocked her head. "You said Mr. Andrews and Matt were there."

"Yeah. After I got out, I spotted them. They took me home."

"Why were they were at the center?"

"Playing tennis, I guess. On the way home, we stopped at his office. Something to do with that hush-hush land deal Matt told us about."

DJ made a face and shook her head. "I knew I shouldn't

have left you alone. You had to go off and play detective while someone trashed this place."

I poked at the pile of cheese, thinking. "Well, I'm not giving up, Deej. This has made me even more worried. It looks like Zola's really in trouble."

"Who knew you would be at the social center?" DJ asked.

"Anna Norberg, for one. The Tuckers could have seen you leave, then followed Anna and me to the center, for two. And Zola's dance pal, Milton, knew I was there."

As I talked, DJ peeled the avocado and put down a slice for each suspect. She added two more. "I hate to say it, but Matt and his Dad sure were close by when you got out."

"So five people either knew I would be there or saw me there. Not much help in narrowing things down."

Waving an arm at the chaos around us, she said, "At least we can't blame Matt or his dad or that friend of Zola's for this mess."

"Unless they had an accomplice."

DJ's face fell. "Oh, yeah. Creepy, isn't it?" She cleared the table and put out a jar of salsa and some napkins.

I checked the pile of grated cheese on the board. It looked like enough. After placing a large flour tortilla in the skillet, I sprinkled the grated cheese on top. As soon as it began to melt, I added a few slices of avocado and folded the tortilla in half, browning the other side, just like Dad used to do. Before it burned, I slipped it onto a plate and did another one.

With the first bite of my quesadilla I closed my eyes, letting the warm cheese ooze across my tongue. To me, anything with melted cheese was pure heaven.

"Mmmm. For a while today, I wasn't sure whether I'd ever eat again."

DJ slumped back in her chair, her eyes narrowed. "Please, promise me—don't go exploring without me anymore. Your mom would kill me if anything happened to you."

Chapter 16

THAT NIGHT I WAS TOO WIRED TO EVEN WATCH TV. Who had shut me in the kiln room? Who had trashed the house? Someone out there must feel threatened enough to spy on us, follow us, and break in. What had I gotten myself into? The whole thing scared me to death, but it also made me determined to end it. Once and for all.

It reminded me of a story Gran used to tell. A tiny mouse wanted to stop a hawk from swooping out of the sky and catching all her relatives. She propped up a pointy stick and piled some brush around it. Then she sat on top of the pile, waiting for the hawk. Sure enough, the hawk came by looking for lunch. Just when the hawk was about to grab her, the mouse dived into the brush, and the hawk speared itself on the pointy stick.

Before going to bed, I spent a few moments with the *David and Goliath* painting. Just like Gran's story, it showed the little guy up against the big guy. Staring at it, I felt a calmness flowing over me, comforting me. Dad was here—not just in the painting, but right here in the room. I felt his spirit close by me, just like Gran had felt about Granddad.

"If someone's out to get me, Dad," I said, "let's hope I'm as quick as that mouse."

I woke in the middle of the night to grumbles of thunder and bright lights flashing outside my window. Unlike the last time I woke up to noises, I knew what these were. Gran used to talk about a summer "monsoon season" here in the desert. This time of year brought wild lightning storms and, with any luck, tons of rain. The thunder grew louder, until it sounded like ten bowling alleys overhead. I gave up on trying to sleep, threw back the covers, transferred to my chair, and went out to the living room. When the lightning flashed, it cast an eerie glow over everything. Sometimes the flashes came so fast they were like cameras going off around a rock star.

Lightning lit up the room again. In the brief seconds of brightness, I noticed the pile of old videos the burglar had dumped next to the television. These were the keepers I'd set aside, the home videos. Special only to us. Pictures of family—Mom, Dad, me . . . Dad! I hurried over, reached down, and fumbled through them, tossing the ones that didn't interest me back into the box. The labels on the sides said things like "Christmas" or "Trip to Disneyland." I finally found the most recent one, the one we made last summer just before the accident.

I turned on the TV and VCR and slipped in the video. The screen flickered, then bathed the room in blue light. There we all were, on the beach at Coronado. The big white hotel loomed like a circus tent in the background. I loved that beach, because the sand sparkled with little gold flakes. It always made me wonder if there was a sunken ship offshore filled with gold coins that were slowly eroding, their flakes washing in with each wave.

Mom and I were kneeling on the sand, hard at work on an elaborate sandcastle. You could tell that Dad, the master sculptor, had helped. Four towers rose from the corners of the walls around the castle. We had dug out a moat and used a flattened soda can for a drawbridge. A sand dragon crouched by the moat, ready to attack.

With her back already red from the sun, Mom turned and waved to the camera. "Hi, Gran! Sorry we couldn't be there for your birthday. Instead of a birthday cake, we made you your very own castle."

Now I waved at the camera. "Just for you, Gran!"

I pulled out a sparkler from our beach bag and stuck it in one of the towers. Mom lit it. While it sputtered with sparks, we all sang "Happy Birthday" to Gran. We sounded a little out of tune but extremely sincere.

The picture tilted. Mom must have taken over recording. Dad came on. Dad—alive, strong, his brown body specked with sand. He flexed his muscles, mugging for the camera.

"*¡Feliz cumpleaños, Mamá!* We'd be with you today to celebrate, but our old Jeep has been giving us trouble. We had it in the shop all week. Something's wrong with the brakes, and we didn't want to risk the long drive across the desert. But we'll be there for Thanksgiving, count on it! Have a great day!" He blew her a kiss.

The video continued with scenes of dolphins leaping out of the water at Sea World, but I wasn't watching anymore. My eyes filled with tears. I stopped the VCR and rewound the tape. I wanted to see Dad again. I needed to hear what he'd said.

". . . giving us trouble. We had it in the shop all week. Something's wrong with the brakes."

It all came rushing back. When Dad got the Jeep back, he thought it was fixed. A week later we took off for our camping trip in the mountains. Like a movie in my head, I could see the road, me pointing at the deer darting up ahead. Dad's foot pumping the brakes. His arms fighting to control the steering. The edge of the road disappearing from underneath us.

Tears of relief rolled down my cheeks. I knew now that the accident hadn't been my fault. If the brakes hadn't failed, Dad would have slowed down. He would have missed the deer, and we would have continued on our way. I let the tears come, feeling the pain wash away with each drop. The room swirled around me, filled with energy, love, and spirits.

For too long, I'd shoved the ache of missing him under a rock in my heart. Now, like the waves at Coronado Beach, all the little moments I'd wished Dad had been there came rolling over me. Maybe he'd been there all along. Like those times I came out of therapy sessions and showed off a new maneuver to Mom. Or when I'd finished reading a great book and wanted to tell someone about it. Or when I'd just wanted to let him know I was okay.

Wiping away my tears, I scanned the room, hoping I could make him appear. "You led me to that video, didn't you?" I whispered, my lips trembling. "You wanted me to know what really happened."

I rewound, pushed the play button, and watched it again.

He blew me a kiss.

Chapter 17

MY DREAMS THAT NIGHT WERE GREAT. I flew high over the world, my arms outstretched like a bird. I floated through billowy clouds, soaring above houses and trees. I woke up happy for the first time in ages. It dawned on me that I'd been carrying around a ton of guilt about the accident. It had squashed my confidence and my spirit, turning me into a shadow of the person I really was. No more. Today I was ready to take on the world.

DJ was already awake, sipping orange juice and reading the morning paper. She looked up when I came in and jabbed her finger at the front page of the *Copper Valley News*.

"Get a load of this!" She pointed to an article, reading it out loud.

"Copper Valley police report their first lead in a string of burglaries plaguing the city. Last night, the Border Patrol stopped a gray panel truck on I-19 for a routine check. The driver sped away, but lost control and rolled the vehicle two miles south of the city, according to police officer Bill Garcia. 'When we arrived on the scene and searched the truck, we found several items matching the description of goods stolen in the recent burglaries,' Garcia said.

"Copper Valley residents have been worried since thieves began taking valuable heirloom jewelry, antique silver sets, and artwork from local homes. Because only one or two items are taken each time, the thefts often go unnoticed for weeks.

"The panel truck driver, a young male, has not been identified, and is under guard at Copper Valley Care Center, where he has been hospitalized with minor injuries. Anyone with information about the thefts is urged to contact police."

DJ shoved the paper toward me. "*¡Vaya!* I thought this was a place where nothing ever happened!"

I thought back on the morning DJ arrived and Zola was over at her house, cleaning up the water. I shook my head, totally amazed at my stupidity. "You know what? I bet I saw that panel truck, right in front of Zola's house.

I just assumed it was the maintenance people. But remember what a mess the house was later? No one ever came to clean up."

DJ's brow furrowed. "Maybe. You can't jump to conclusions. There could be lots of gray panel trucks around here. It doesn't mean the one in the wreck was the one you saw."

"No, but it could be. Gran's neighborhood isn't so quiet, either. The other night somebody was making a racket outside at three in the morning. Voices, pounding noises, then tires squealing down the street."

"If there's a law against driving down a street in the middle of the night, then a whole lot of people are in trouble," DJ said.

"Maybe Zola saw the burglar breaking in somewhere. Maybe he came back and grabbed her to shut her up." I folded the paper and thought a moment. "You know what we should do?"

DJ looked at me warily. "What?"

"Talk to that guy in the hospital. Maybe he knows something about Zola."

"You mean the panel truck driver?" She frowned and shook her head. "Uh-uh. No way."

"Why not?"

"He's got no reason to talk to us. And besides, I don't think the police would be too happy about a couple of girls flouncing in for a nice bedside chat."

"But they want the public's help. It says so right there in the paper."

She snorted. "They want people who can give information."

I waved her off. "Whatever. We'll say we're his relatives. What have we got to lose? It's worth a try, Deej."

She sighed and rolled her eyes to the ceiling. "I suppose I better say okay, or you'll just plow ahead without me and get yourself in trouble again."

I grinned at her. "I knew you'd see it my way!"

As we headed out the drive, the Tuckers were back at it, loading up their van for another swap meet. Frankly, I'd rather go to the mall and get brand new stuff than walk around in the hot sun looking at other people's junk. Today the wind was kicking up, too, blowing dust and making a ride in a convertible no fun. DJ pulled over after a couple of blocks and put the top up. She checked the map against the address we had for the Copper Valley Care Center and found it was near the center of town, not far away.

Starting off again, she asked, "Do you have any idea what you'll ask this guy?"

"Not yet. I'm thinking."

She hushed up and drove on, glancing now and then in the rear-view mirror. Suddenly she turned right, away from the hospital. I grabbed for the dashboard as my whole body careened sideways.

"Hey, take it easy! Where are you going?"

"I'm not sure. Maybe I'm getting paranoid, but I think someone's following us."

"Well, no sudden turns or stops, okay? I can't brace myself with my legs, remember?"

She flashed me an apologetic look. "Gee. Sorry. I keep forgetting."

I checked the rear-view mirror on my side. A white van trailed several yards behind us. Sunglasses and a baseball cap hid the driver's face. "It looks a lot like the Tuckers' van. But they should be going north to Tucson if they were swap-meeting again."

"It reminds me of that guy who almost hit us yesterday on the way to see Matt's land." DJ turned right again, slower this time. Two more turns and we were back on the road to the hospital. The van stayed behind, even though a blue car was now between us. An icy sweat ran down my neck. I was starting to think DJ was right. But why would someone follow us?

When we pulled into the hospital parking lot, the white van sailed on by. A sign on the side read "Buckeye Hardware." DJ glanced at me and shrugged. "Not the Tuckers after all. They don't have a sign on their van."

"Maybe Mr. Buckeye thought we were a couple of cute babes," I said, hoping that was all there was to it.

The Copper Valley Care Center wasn't big like the hospitals in Tucson or San Diego. It was more like the clinic where I'd done my physical therapy. Gran had told me that all the serious medical cases, like heart surgery, were taken by ambulance or helicopter up to Tucson. She had hoped she'd never have to spend time in either place. As things turned out, her illness took her quietly in her own home.

The lobby was a cool relief from the dusty heat outside. It was done in soothing shades of blue and lavender, with desert murals painted on the walls. But the cozy decor couldn't hide the antiseptic smell. I wrinkled my nose. It brought back bad memories.

We asked at the information desk about the guy who'd been in the accident. Without batting an eye, the clerk directed us to Room 215. So far, so good. I still had no idea how this was going to work. My heart boinged like a wire spring. We both kept glancing around, watching for anyone who might be spying on us or following us.

Outside the door of Room 215, an old guy sat in a tan uniform, reading a paperback novel. He looked more like hospital security than police.

DJ stopped a few doors short of the guard. "Now what, genius?"

I pushed toward the guard. "Come on. We came all this way to see if this guy was our long-lost cousin, didn't we?"

The guard looked up as we approached.

"Excuse me," I said, "can we speak to the man inside?"

He put his book down, stood up, and eyed us doubtfully. "That depends. What's your interest?"

"We think he may be our cousin," I explained.

"What's your name?"

"Ramos. Crystal Ramos. This is my sister, Dolores." DJ glared down at me for using her real name.

"Let me see if he's awake. He's been in and out." The guard ducked inside and quickly came back out. "He's awake, but good luck talking to him. He don't speak English, only Spanish. I can't understand a thing he says."

I nudged DJ.

"That's okay. I speak Spanish," she said, picking up her cue.

The guard pushed open the door and followed us in. "Well, good luck, ladies."

A single bed occupied the pale blue hospital room. There were no flowers and no get-well cards. A soccer game blinked silently from an overhead TV. The guy in the bed looked pretty banged up. A bandage covered his forehead and left eye. The area around his right eye was black and blue, and one leg was slightly suspended in a half cast.

"You got visitors, señor," said the guard, leaning against the door, his arms folded.

The guy slowly turned his head our way. He was

110

young, maybe in his twenties. A sly smile spread under his thin mustache, like he really was our cousin and was happy to see us.

I pushed my chair over to the head of the bed, so DJ could come in close. She fumbled with the edge of her T-shirt. "*Hola*, Umm . . . *¿Cómo está?*"

Grinning, he reached out and grabbed DJ's hand. "*¡Hola chula! ¡Dame un beso!*"

I bit my lip, trying not to giggle. He'd called DJ a "cutie," and had asked for a kiss.

DJ pulled her hand away, but kept smiling, watching the guard's reaction to all this. His face stayed blank, so she continued. "*Por favor, ¿conoce a Zola?*"

The guy's smile faded, and his dark eyes narrowed. "*Vieja metiche,*" he sneered, as spit flew across the sheet.

DJ glanced over at me. I shrugged, not understanding what he'd said. She leaned forward, crooning sweetly like she was asking a child where it hurt. "*Ay, pobrecito. ¿Dónde está Zola?*"

Turning away, he closed his eyes. "*No sé, no sé.*"

"*¿Dónde está Zola?*" DJ demanded.

No answer.

"*¿Cómo se llama usted?*"

He pushed her away and muttered "*¡No más!*" It was clear that the interview was over.

As we started for the door, the guard stopped us. "Well, what'd he say? Is that your cousin?"

DJ shrugged. "He wasn't making much sense." She glanced back at the guy in the bed. "It's hard to recognize him all bandaged up like that. Maybe we'd better come back another day."

"You do that," the guard said, a tinge of suspicion in his voice. His hand slipped into his pocket and pulled out a cell phone.

For once, I let DJ push my chair down the hallway, so we could get out of there faster. When we were out in the lobby again, I made her stop.

"What'd he say? I couldn't get it all."

"I asked if he knew Zola. You know what he called her?"

"What?"

"A meddling old lady! A busybody."

I laughed. "Maybe he was calling *you* that!"

"I don't think so. Notice how he stopped flirting when I brought up her name? When I asked where she was, he said he didn't know. He also wouldn't tell me his name. But I think we got what we came for. A connection."

As soon as we left the parking lot, a white van pulled out and started tailing us again. I glanced in the side mirror. It sure looked like the same one, but since every other vehicle in southern Arizona was white, it could have been anyone. Still, it made me nervous. Arizona cars have no front license plates, so unless the guy passed us we couldn't get the number. Two blocks from the street that led into our neighborhood, the van turned off.

Chapter 18

A KID ON A RED-AND-SILVER BICYCLE was making lazy loops on our street. DJ was about to honk at him, but she hesitated. "Is that Matt?"

"Looks like him."

She slowed down and eased the car alongside him. "Hi! That the bike from the pawn shop?"

He beamed at us, circled around the car, and stopped. Pulling off his helmet, he said, "Like it? Dad bought it for me this morning. What are you two doing?"

I pushed my palms down on the seat and boosted myself up, so I could see the bike. "Not much. We've just been visiting a burglar."

Matt's eyes widened. "A burglar? You went to a jail?"

"He's in the care center, actually," said DJ. "We found out he knows Zola."

Matt let out a low whistle. "She was hanging around with thieves?"

"No, dummy. We think she saw something suspicious, maybe even the burglar himself. We think there's a connection between the robberies around here and Zola's disappearance."

"It's like a puzzle," I explained. "Each piece tells us something. Zola's photos told us she was interested in patios. The fact that she left her overnight case behind says she's not really off on a trip. Someone ransacked our house yesterday. And the burglar knew who she was."

"Wow, really?" He jerked his thumb toward Gran's house. "I saw the cops come yesterday. I wanted to see what was going on, but Dad wouldn't let me."

I turned to DJ. "You know, we should talk to Zola's friend Milton again. He said he'd been asking around about Zola. Maybe he's learned something new."

"Hey, I know him," said Matt, giving his helmet a tap. "The old guy with orange hair? He's in my lapidary class."

I nodded. "That's him."

"Any idea where we can find him?" asked DJ.

Matt stared at the ground, thinking. "What's today? Thursday? I bet he's at the craft fair at the social center."

DJ started the car. "Worth a try. See you!"

The parking lot at the West Hills Center was jammed with cars, even down the side streets. A huge sign by the entrance announced CRAFT FAIR TODAY, 9 TO 5. DJ dropped me off and went to hunt for a parking place. While I waited for her, I wheeled past the displays lining the sidewalks. Knitted shawls, glazed pottery, jewelry, wooden birdhouses, and handwoven place mats and rugs covered the tables. It wasn't junk, either. I found myself eyeing things that might make a good present for Mom when she got back.

Dozens of customers clustered around each table, some buying, others just chatting. I scanned the crowd. Sure enough, over by the fountain, I spotted a fuzzy head of orange hair. DJ trotted over to join me.

Milton looked surprised to see me there. "How-dee-do!" He held out his hand to DJ. "Don't think we've met."

"This is my cousin, DJ," I said hurriedly.

"Got some nice baubles here for you," Milton said.

I glanced at the jewelry spread out on his table. A silver butterfly pin caught my eye. The wings were set with dark polished stones. They shimmered with the iridescent colors of real butterfly wings.

"What kind of stone is this?" I asked.

"Spectrolite. Comes all the way from Finland. Don't look like much till it's polished up. You like it?"

"It's nice," I said, putting the pin back down next to a pair of amethyst earrings. "But actually, we came to ask you a couple of questions."

"About Zola," added DJ.

Milton's brow wrinkled as he pulled out a soft cloth and started polishing a silver bracelet with coral inlay. "I'm still worried about her. Any news yet?"

"We called the police," I said. "A cop came by, then talked to us and the neighbors. Her neighbor claims she went off with her brother to the Grand Canyon."

Milton shook his head. "That don't make no sense. No sirree. She said her brother wasn't in very good shape. Someone else must've come for her—maybe some friend of her brother's." He plopped down on a chair behind his table and put on a wide-brimmed straw hat.

Wearing that hat, Milton reminded me of someone. At first I couldn't remember, but then it hit me. "You're the one I saw coming out of Zola's house with a sack of something, aren't you," I said, pointing at him. "Did you take her purse?"

He looked offended. "Take it? No ma'am. I stopped by with some groceries, but she was gone. Found the door open, so I checked inside. She never went anywhere without that purse. Seein' it there and her gone, I got worried. I stuck it in her closet out of sight."

"You straightened up in there, too, didn't you?" asked DJ.

"Yup. Zola always keeps her place real tidy-like. It sure bothered me, finding her door open and the place a mess.

Anyone could've grabbed her stuff. And she was always goin' on about someone stealing things in the neighborhood."

"Did she say who?" I asked.

Milton rubbed his chin, thinking. "No. She skipped right by the who part. Started talking about the swimming pool behind her place. Didn't make much sense at the time. But the other day, I poked around and found an empty chlorine bucket in the oleander hedge."

My memory clicked. "Matt told us the pool was closed because it had too much chlorine in it. Why would someone do that?"

Milton traced a square on the cloth covering his table. "Here's the pool. Three houses run close by, including Zola's. An empty pool would sure cut down the chances of anyone seein' something they shouldn't."

DJ and I exchanged looks. More pieces of the puzzle were falling into place. But a big piece was still missing. Before we left, I thanked Milton and bought the butterfly pin for Mom. He beamed at me like I'd made his whole day.

Chapter 19

BY THE TIME WE GOT BACK TO GRAN'S HOUSE, dark thunderclouds were billowing up again from the south, making the sky look like an angry sea. A brisk breeze jangled the wind chimes on the patio, sending a nervous melody through the air. My uneasiness returned as I stared at Zola's empty house. At about six-thirty, the phone rang. I grabbed it, hoping it was Mom.

"This is Rustam," a voice announced in an accent. "I am brother to Zola. Are you Crystal?"

"Yes." I waved my arm frantically for DJ to come closer.

"We are at Tucson airport. I must fly to Chicago tonight. Can you come to get Zola and bring her back home?"

"Tucson airport? Sure." I covered the receiver and whispered, "It's Zola's brother!"

I returned to the caller. "Can you put Zola on the phone?"

"Umm . . . she is in lavatory. Can you come now? To the West Air counter?"

"Yes, okay. Tell her we'll be there in forty-five minutes."

"Is Zola all right?" asked DJ after I hung up.

"I guess so. Her brother, or whoever that was, said he had to return to Chicago right away. He asked if we could come pick her up at the West Air counter."

DJ made a face. "I bet. Where was Zola?"

"In the ladies' room, or so he said."

"Do you think that was really her brother?"

"Well, he had an odd foreign name. *Roostam*, I think he said. And he spoke with an accent, sort of like Zola does. We have to go, Deej, in case she's there. Maybe we can finally find out what happened."

DJ grabbed her keys. "Fine with me." She hesitated. "Something about that call doesn't sound right, whether or not it was really her brother. I can't put my finger on it."

"I wish I could have heard Zola's voice. Then we'd be sure."

Outside, a low rumble of thunder confirmed that a storm was coming. The wall of clouds to the south had turned dark blue. The sun wouldn't set for another hour, but already the daylight was gone. Before getting into DJ's car, I glanced up at the sky. The desert air felt alive with static electricity. Pale lights flickered in the clouds overhead, and I felt a shiver of foreboding.

"Deej, how about if we split up? You go to the airport and get Zola—if she's there. I'll stay here. Something tells me one of us should stick around."

DJ pursed her lips, shaking her head slowly. "I don't know. The last time I left you on your own, you almost got cooked."

"I'll be okay. If things get crazy, I'll call the cops. Promise."

With a sigh, she conceded. "You are one stubborn *chica*." As she slid behind the wheel, she said, "I guess we have no choice. I'm the one with the car, so I have to check out this airport call. You stay out of trouble, okay? I'll be back as soon as I can."

"You better hurry. Maybe you can beat the storm as you head north."

"I'll leave my cell phone on," DJ said as she turned the key in the ignition. "Call me if you need me."

"Yeah, okay. Go!"

After DJ left, I lingered on the driveway for a few minutes, considering my next move. The whole neighborhood seemed to be holding its breath. Across the street, the

Tuckers' townhouse was dark, their carport vacant.

I reached behind into my backpack and pulled out the envelope of photos. One by one I studied them again. My pulse quickened. The photo with the young man cleaning the golf clubs caught my attention. His thin mustache made him look kind of familiar. Was he the same guy DJ and I had seen today in the care center? And whose patio was it? One of the golf bags was resting across a chair. I checked the photo of the Tuckers' patio again. There was the same chair, the one with the tattered webbing. But now the golf clubs were gone, the boxes in the background, too. Seeing the man there must have thrown us off and made us think it was his patio. If he was the same guy from the rollover, that meant the Tuckers knew him. Was this the photo that got Zola in trouble?

More questions buzzed in my head. Susan Tucker's comment about living with so much stuff that they could hardly turn around came back to me. And didn't Anna Norberg say something about their place being crowded with things? If they had so much, why did Zola's photo of their patio show nothing there? Was their house empty, too?

My mind made up, I pushed myself across the street. Somehow, I had to get a look inside the Tuckers' townhouse. I guess Gran had been right about me. I do like to plunge into things.

The blinds in their front window were closed tight, so

I scooted over to the side door by the carport. Skimpy half-curtains hung in the door's small window, giving me a partial view of the inside. Boosting myself up from my chair, I strained to peek in. A hall light cast a dim glow inside.

It wasn't what I saw that surprised me, but what I didn't see. Instead of a house jammed full of furniture, the place looked bare. No kitchen table. No chairs. No junk. No stolen loot. I craned my neck, trying to see into the living room. No furniture there, either, as far as I could tell. How could they live like that? I thought back on how Mrs. Tucker wouldn't let me in when I came asking about Zola. Had she been trying to hide the fact that their house was nearly empty? DJ's comment about the photos haunted me, too. *Maybe the clue is what isn't there . . .*

The sound of an approaching car snapped me to attention. Quickly, I wheeled myself to the end of the carport and ducked around a tall oleander hedge. Behind me, the walkway stretched to the neighborhood pool and cabana. Just as I got settled, the Tuckers' white van pulled into the carport.

I held my breath as my heart thumped in my chest. Overhead, palm branches flapped in the wind, scolding me for being a peeping Tomasina. Ward and Susan Tucker said nothing to each other as they climbed out. Susan disappeared into their house. Ward pulled a magnetic sign off the side of the van and carried it inside. The words "Buckeye Hardware" made my eyebrows jump.

A web of lightning streaked across the sky. Seconds later, thunder growled. I wondered how long I could stay hidden. At any moment, the skies would open up. The spicy scent of rain was already in the air.

The side door opened and the Tuckers hustled out, carrying suitcases. They went inside again and returned with more suitcases. They argued about something. I cupped my hand by my ear, trying to hear what they were saying, but the wind sucked their voices away.

Then Susan Tucker turned abruptly and headed across the street as the first raindrops started to fall. Mr. Tucker climbed into the van and started the engine. Headlights flashed on, blinding me with their glare. I ducked, hoping the hedge had hidden me. It hadn't.

Too late, I realized that the metal spokes of my wheel-chair were sparkling like a Christmas tree in the bright lights. A door slammed, and I froze as "Santa" strode right toward me, cursing as he came.

Chapter 20

WARD TUCKER EXPLODED THROUGH the oleander bushes, eyes bulging in anger. His fat face glistened in the bursts of lightning. His rain-splattered shirt clung to his arms as he shook his fist at me.

"I've had enough of your snooping around where you don't belong!" he shouted over the storm. "Why aren't you at the Tucson airport?"

I eased backwards, hoping to escape. "I decided not to go."

He grabbed my chair, stopping me. "Bad move."

"Where's Zola?" I demanded.

He jerked his head. "Across the street. Susan's getting

her now. She's been in that vacant house. She's been right next door to you the whole time!"

"Why? What did she ever do to you?"

"She got nosy. As long as she was just yapping nonsense about 'things going missing,' no one believed her. But then she started taking pictures."

"But you never got them. We did."

A flicker of blue light danced along the fence, snapping with electricity. He eyed it nervously, his fingers working a scorpion clasp down his black bola tie.

"I figured you had the photos when I couldn't find them in your grandmother's place." Abruptly, he grabbed my hands.

"Let go of me!" I yelled, trying to pull away.

He slipped the leather tie from his neck, lashing my wrists together in one swift move. Planting his face right in front of mine, he snarled, "Now I need to stash you, too, missy. At least for a while." Grabbing my chair, he shoved it backwards toward the cabana area. I glanced around, searching for a way to escape. There wasn't any. He was in total control.

The back of my chair slammed against the pool gate. The POOL CLOSED sign clattered above me on the chain-link fencing. I hoped his plan, whatever that was, had failed. But no. He fished out a lock pick from his pocket and went to work on the padlock. He grinned down at me, his fat cheeks shiny.

"Used to be in the hardware business, back in Ohio. Sold keys. Opened locks for customers. It came in real handy for getting into houses."

I tugged at my hands, trying to gulp back the helpless feeling that threatened to turn me to jelly. *Stall for time,* I thought. *Maybe someone will come.* I glared back at him. "That bucket of chlorine came in handy, too, didn't it? You dumped it in the pool to keep people away. No swimmers to look over the fence and see the stolen goods on your patio, or to watch you clearing out your house. You didn't expect Zola to mess up your plan, did you?"

He ignored the question. The gate swung open and he waltzed us through to the cabana area, still pushing me backwards. Now the rain came down in sheets. A streak of lightning sizzled across the sky, turning the curtain of water to silver streaks. I cringed at the sight of the dark pool, which now looked more like a black lagoon. *Nooo. Not there,* I pleaded silently.

He stopped suddenly, and I nearly tumbled out of my chair. "I got to think what to do with you to keep you quiet."

"Why are you doing this? What about Zola?"

"Me and the missus are hightailing it into Mexico. We'll drop Zola at the border. By the time the authorities find her and figure out who she is, we'll be long gone. No one will understand her babbling story. We'll be all settled in, *muy feliz,* in a palm-shaded *casita* on the coast."

The thunder rumbled so loud I had to shout. "But why? Why the thefts? Why run to Mexico?"

"Money, my dear, money. You plan all your life for retirement, but it's never enough. So to add to the pot, we decided to 'borrow' a few goodies from our rich neighbors."

"You sold that kind of stuff at the swap meet?"

He threw back his head and laughed, making his belly jiggle. Like Santa. An evil, demented Santa. "No, my dear. We never went to any stinking swap meets. We sold everything through a buddy we had helping us. He's the one who grabbed Zola and stashed her later that night. Then the fool got careless and crashed. We'd hoped to make our nest egg bigger, but Zola and you made us move up our schedule. For that, you owe me."

I didn't even want to think what the payment might be. I prayed it wouldn't land me in the pool. Anywhere but in the water. Memories from the accident came rushing back. Panic welled up in me, and I started yelling. "Stop! Help! Someone help me!"

The sky bristled again with lightning. A split second later, thunder exploded.

"No one can hear you over this storm!" he shouted. "Ours is the closest house. Too bad we aren't home!" He pushed me out into the rain and parked me near the edge of the pool. My wheels bumped against the curved tile border. Rain drummed the cement. My heart pounded. I feared what might be next. This guy was nuts, for sure.

"You just sit tight, little lady. If you're lucky, you won't get zapped by some lightning bolt."

As he spoke, more sparks flickered and snapped along the fence. Long tendrils of blue light snaked across the wet pavement toward us. I gripped my armrest, bracing for an electric shock. Mr. Tucker let go of my chair.

"Wh-what the Sam Hill?" He turned to run from the blue light, snagging his foot on one of my wheels. Tugging hard, he tried to free himself, but when he did, my chair tipped.

The world turned upside down as I toppled sideways into the pool. Cold water slapped my face, then sucked me under. My nose filled until I blew out a few bubbles and held my breath. My hands twisted under the tie. Finally, I worked them free. Now I had a little more control, but heart-stabbing fear was pulling me down, down toward the bottom. I could sense a throbbing in my ears, like some message was trying to get through. Then I heard it. *Relax. Relax. Relaaaax.*

I shifted my thoughts from going down to going limp. I felt my body begin to rise slowly. If I could only hold my breath long enough, I might be okay. My eyes stung, and my chest ached for air. I counted. *One, one thousand. Two, one thousand. Still rising. Three, one thousand. Four . . . Keep going, keep going,* I told myself.

When I broke the surface, I gasped. Then I froze in fear. Was Mr. Tucker still there? I held myself still, listening.

Fat raindrops thrummed on my back.

Play dead. Play dead, a new message urged.

I didn't need to tell the lower half of my body to play dead. It was dead. My body stayed limp, my head down and my arms floating out like wings. But how long could I stay this way? Two minutes? Three minutes? Five? Finally, I had to peek. I had to know.

Slowly, I turned my head, peering out through strands of hair. My wheelchair lay at the edge of the pool, dumped on its side. My seat cushion bobbed in the water nearby. Footsteps slapped through the puddles. I saw a figure slip through the gate and heard it clang shut. With my hands doing tiny dog-paddles, I drifted over to the steps leading out of the pool. My eyes stung from the chlorine. My skin prickled like I'd fallen into a bed of cactus. I had to get out of the water. On my own. Then, somehow, I had to get back to my chair. Get it turned upright. Get back into it.

A voice whispered inside my head. *You can do it, Ranita, remember? Way back when you were in physical therapy? One of your lessons was about getting back in your chair if you fell. It was hard, but you did it.*

I remembered, and I smiled, feeling Dad's presence urging me on. Sure, I'd done an exercise like this before. But that was from a nice hard floor. And there was always someone there to give me a hand if I needed it. I never had to do it like this, all alone, from a swimming pool.

My fingertips brushed the rough edge of a step. Good, almost there. I followed the step over to the chrome railing that led down into the water. Once I grasped the cool metal, I felt connected to the world again. My head jerked upward, and I took a big gulp of air. Hanging tightly to the rail, I pulled into a sitting position on the top step. Next, I propped both hands behind me and heaved my body up over the edge and onto the deck. I glanced around to see where I'd landed. The rain had ended, leaving huge puddles of water everywhere. The scent of mesquite and creosote filled the air, and flashes of lightning still pulsed in distant clouds. My toppled wheelchair lay about ten feet away. Not far from it was a lounge chair. Good, I thought. That's my first goal.

Inch by inch, I scooched across the rough cement on my butt, dragging my legs. Thankfully it was dark, and the deck wasn't burning hot. Even so, my hands and feet oozed blood from being scraped. When I reached the lounge chair, I grabbed the leg and pulled it along until it was positioned parallel to my wheelchair. So far, so good.

With both hands, I grasped the plastic straps that crisscrossed the frame of the lounge. The chair tipped forward under my weight, but I kept going, hauling myself onto it, arm over arm. Finally, the lounge leveled out again. I lay there for a few moments, panting and giving my muscles a rest. *Almost there. Almost done.*

I rolled over and pushed myself up. The big spoked

wheel of my chair was only a few inches away. Trying not to lose my balance, I tugged at the wheel until the chair rose and righted itself with a clatter. Now for the hard part. How had I done this in therapy? First, set the brakes. Now move the armrest out of the way. Grab the far armrest with the left arm. Got it? Use your right arm to shove your body off, pull, and . . . over!

I landed with a grunt, sitting a little lopsided, but home again in my seat. Now that I was in my chair, I felt in control again. But I was also mad. Real mad. What a creep to leave me to drown in that pool!

Voices from the street told me the Tuckers were still out there. Maybe Zola, too. I still had a chance to do something. In his dash to get away, Mr. Tucker had left the pool gate unlocked. I sped through the cabana and around the oleander hedge. The clouds overhead parted, and a full moon shone down on me. My arms, neck, and head felt cold and tingly. I caught a glimpse of my reflection in a puddle of water. In the moonlight, my wet skin and clothes glistened like silver. But the best part was my hair. It stood out in a frizzy blue glow, like I'd stuck my finger in a light socket. I knew Dad was surrounding me with his presence.

The Tuckers had backed their van across the street and into the carport of the vacant house. I was surprised they were still there. Then I saw why. Milton had parked his golf cart right in front their van, blocking their escape. He and Mr. Tucker were arguing.

"What's your big hurry?" Milton demanded. "I got more questions. I heard some shouting a few minutes ago, and I'm thinkin' it might have been Zola. What have you done with her?"

I kept closing in on them. So far, no one had noticed me.

Ward Tucker grabbed Milton by the arm and pushed him over to his golf cart. "You're just looking for trouble, aren't you?" he growled. "Now get a move on before you get more than you bargained for."

Milton jerked his arm away and stumbled against his cart. "Hey, back off! What are you two doin' over here, anyway? This ain't your house. You're acting like—"

"W-W-Ward. Look!" Susan blubbered, scrambling out of the van and over to her husband. Her face pale, she pointed her finger at me. I was now in the middle of the street.

Mr. Tucker turned, his eyes wide. I'm sure he thought I was a silver ghost. He blinked and shook his head.

"Go away! You're dead." He shoved his wife toward their van. "Get in, Susan!"

They bolted into the van. It lurched across the gravel yard, smashed through a clump of cactus, and bumped out into the street.

"No!" I shouted to Milton, who stood by his cart looking stunned. "They're getting away!"

Then a flash of headlights barreling toward us caught my eye. A turquoise convertible screeched to a sideways stop, blocking their escape down the street. DJ hopped out, picked up a rock, and hurled it, smashing the van's windshield.

Mr. Tucker beat his fist on the steering wheel. He backed up, swung the van around, and aimed his lights right at me. My heart leaped to my throat. If he figured I was a ghost and already dead, driving through me wouldn't matter a bit. But I wasn't a ghost. I was solid flesh and blood.

Instinctively, I tilted my chair back, doing a wheelie and hoping—praying—that he'd miss me. DJ launched another rock, a perfect fastball pitch. This one smacked the side window, making the van swerve. As it did, the fender clipped my footrest, sending me tumbling backwards. Things happened in slow motion as I fell. Before my head met the pavement, I heard screaming. A metallic crash. A blaring horn. Then pain exploded like fireworks in my head.

Chapter 21

DAD AND I STOOD BY A CRYSTAL BLUE LAKE, surrounded by thick blue spruce. A clear sky arched overhead, reflected on the water's surface below. We'd each caught three rainbow trout for dinner. It was perfect. Too perfect.

"Let's call it a day, okay, Ranita?" Dad reeled in his line and started to pack up our gear. "See if you can find some firewood. I'll clean the fish."

I trotted over to a mountain of driftwood piled up at the edge of the lake. The branches, worn smooth by wind and water, were completely dry—perfect for a fire.

"Is this enough?" I knelt down and dumped my armload

by the circle of stones we had arranged at our campsite.

"That's fine for now." In no time, Dad had the pile crackling with fire. I ran over to the Jeep and grabbed the cooler. Mom had packed salad, hard-boiled eggs, chocolate cake, sodas, and even a can of tuna in case we didn't catch anything.

As we waited for the flames to die back, Dad clinked his soda can against mine.

"Finally, we get to finish our camping trip. It's been a long time, Ranita."

"Yeah. I've missed you," I said, putting my head on his shoulder.

He mussed my hair gently. "I've missed you, too. I'm glad to see you can take care of yourself. I don't feel so bad now about leaving you."

"You felt bad? Why?"

"Because of what happened to your back! And then you went around with a long face, thinking it was all your fault."

"But it was just an accident, wasn't it."

He smiled. "Yes. Just one of those stupid things. Not my fault. Not your fault. So stop beating up on yourself, okay?"

"I promise, Daddy."

He gave a quick smile. "I have to go now, Ranita."

I gave him a hug. "Can we do this again? I like these visits."

"Sure thing, Ranita."

A bright light flooded the scene at the lake, making the blue sky, the lake, the trees, and Dad all fade away. I wanted him back. I heard myself shouting, "Daddy! Daddy!"

"It's okay, Crystal. Shhh. You were dreaming."

It wasn't Dad's voice. I opened my eyes. A blinding light shone right in my face. I blocked it with my arm and saw two figures standing by my bed. All I could make out were dark shapes in a halo of light.

"Where am I? Am I dead?"

DJ muffled a laugh. "No, not quite. But you had us scared for a while. You're in the Copper Valley Care Center. You've got a little concussion, plus a bad rash from being in that swimming pool."

I reached up and felt a thick bandage covering a large lump on the back of my head. "Oww!" I cried.

"Easy now." Matt's voice cut in as he leaned closer. It was nice to see his freckled face again. "You shook up old Mr. Tucker so much that he crashed into our carport. He totaled my dad's golf cart. You watch, Dad's going to sue him!"

I looked over at DJ. "I remember your car. You came charging in just like the cavalry. What made you come back?"

DJ grinned. "You know how I said there was something odd about that phone call from Zola's so-called brother? I was halfway to Tucson when it hit me. There are no West Air flights from Tucson to Chicago at night. I know because this spring the softball team had a game in Chicago. The last flight out is at noon. I called the airlines from the road to be sure. Then I called the cops."

My head still hurt, but things were coming back to me. "What about Zola? Is she all right?"

"A little bruised, but fine," said DJ. "She was in the back of the van when it crashed."

"And the Tuckers?"

"In the pokey for now," said Matt with a grin. "They're in a whole pile of trouble. What were they up to, anyway?"

I closed my eyes, which were still burning from the chorine, and tried to put some order to my thoughts. My memories were all jumbled up with scenes from my dream. "I remember Mr. Tucker saying they needed money. He'd been breaking into houses and stealing things. Zola and her camera really set him off."

"And that guy in the panel truck fenced the stuff?" asked DJ.

"Yeah. They were going to disappear into Mexico after they dumped Zola at the border. It was their own cushy retirement plan."

"Well, now they can retire in Florence, in the state pen." DJ said. She sighed and looked at the ceiling. "Who knew this geezer town would turn out to be Crime Central?"

"What about Mom?"

DJ put her hand on my arm. "We had to call her to get you admitted here. She's on her way right now. I told her you'd be okay, but she was pretty upset, anyway."

I suddenly felt very tired. "Great. Now she'll never let me be on my own again. She'll be watching my every move."

As if on cue, Mom swept into the room and threw her arms around me, hugging me close.

Chapter 22

WHEN MOM PICKED ME UP FROM THE HOSPITAL the next day, I thought we'd go straight to Gran's place. Instead, she pulled into Zola's carport.

"She wants to see you," Mom said, smiling over at me.

"Good. I want to make sure she's okay, too."

A burst of cheers greeted me when I came through the door. Far from looking normal and tidy, Zola's place rocked like a New Year's Eve party. There were streamers, balloons, and flowers everywhere. Neighbors and friends filled the living room and the kitchen, and DJ and Matt tooted at me with party horns.

Zola came scurrying over, wearing her frilly dance

class dress. Except for a dark bruise on her arm, she looked like her old self. She bent down, cupped my face in her knobby hands, and kissed my cheek.

"Here is my brave little friend!" she said. "You are okay now?"

"Yes, I'm fine. How about you?"

"Good as new." She gave my cheek a pat. "Come. Meet my new helper, Myra."

She motioned over a young woman who was dressed in a casual pink uniform. She reminded me of my third-grade teacher—friendly, but also strict. I shook Myra's hand. "Are you a nurse?"

"Health aide. I'll be here during the day and on call at night."

Zola nodded toward Horace Andrews, who was sitting on the sofa. "Is big lawyer's idea. So I don't get in more trouble!"

"And how did you get in trouble this time?"

Zola waved her hands in disgust. "I know something is going on next door, but I have no proof. So I borrow little camera and start taking pictures. He sees me, I see him, and I hide film quick. Some man comes right in my house asking for camera. So I give." She giggled at the memory. "'Sure. Take camera,' I say. 'Now go!' But does he go? No. He grabs me. When I wake up, I am locked in empty house."

DJ handed me a cold drink. "They kept her knocked

out most of the time with drugs. But when they came to take her away, the drugs had worn off. They had their hands full trying to get her into that van."

Zola winked at me. "First I fight. Then I pretend I am dead. Go limp, like in old days of Viet Nam war protests. I am not so dumb. Have to buy time for someone—for you and my boyfriend—to save me. How do I thank you, my little friend?"

I squeezed her hand. "Just stay well. And don't give Myra any grief."

"I'll see that she behaves herself," said Milton. He ambled over to take Zola's hand and led her to a chair. "We got lots to talk about," he added.

After Zola and Milton left us, I gazed across the living room, watching Mom as she visited with everyone. I had the feeling the neighbors, including Anna Norberg, were talking about me and filling her in on what had happened. Every now and then she'd look over at me with her eyes wide, like she was saying, "My daughter did *that?*"

Through the crowd, I spotted Matt on the patio. He caught my eye and waved me outside.

"Come on, Deej," I said, grabbing her arm. "I still have a few questions for Matt about his so-called ranch."

Today, Matt looked like a junior version of his dad. He wore khaki pants, a blue golf shirt, and loafers. He was perched on a patio chair, trying to balance a plate of snacks and a drink. "Nice party, huh?" he said, flashing me his best smile. "DJ and I decorated."

"You did great. I'm sorry about suspecting your dad. He was being awfully secretive."

Matt shrugged it off. "Yeah, but that's all out in the open now. He'd heard that some company was planning a big development for the land we looked at. Not crowded like most are these days, but with small ranches and lots of open space for wildlife. He wanted to be sure he got a piece of the deal before the prices jumped."

Matt put his plate on the ground. He stood up and dug into his pocket, coming up with a small card. "Here's my dad's business card. Not because you need a lawyer. I wrote my e-mail address on the bottom. Let me know when you come back and get settled."

"Settled?" I stared at him and then at DJ, confused.

DJ squatted down next to me. "Your mom and I had a long talk last night about the possibility of you two moving into Gran's place."

Matt sat down and picked up his snacks. "Yeah. You could go to school just down the road in Rio Vista. I bet I could talk my old man into letting me come to visit more often. Between the two of us, we could lower the average age around here by at least a couple of decades!"

I let these new ideas sink in for a moment. "It's tempting," I admitted. "But how could Mom decide all this without even talking to me?"

"Relax. It's not decided," said DJ. "She promised she'd

discuss the whole plan with you before she makes any decisions."

And she did. Later that afternoon, Mom and I got out a yellow tablet and made a list of all the pros and cons about moving into Gran's place. On the plus side was all the money we'd save. Also, her show was doing so well in Santa Fe that they wanted more of her work. We'd be a whole lot closer to the gallery here than in San Diego. Mom started to put "new school" down on the negative side, but I stopped her. The idea of starting out in a new place was growing on me. It had all kinds of good possibilities, including seeing Matt once in a while.

The next day, while Mom loaded the car for our trip back to San Diego, I sat out on the patio, listening to Gran's wind chime. A fat quail waddled along the back fence, stopping now and then to chirp out a message. From somewhere not far away, another quail answered. *Wip-wip, wip-wip.*

In my lap, I cradled the watercolor of Dad. The painting was back in its silver frame where it belonged. DJ and I figured Mr. Tucker had let himself into Gran's place and had stolen the frame, thinking it was more valuable than the painting. By the time anyone found the painting under the bed, he and the missus would be long gone. Then he must have panicked and thought that by giving back the frame, he'd look innocent.

I hadn't told Mom about the videos. There was time

enough. We'd have ourselves a "family reunion film festival" after we got settled. My bruised heart was finally starting to mend. I had found Zola, and that lost piece of myself, too. The accident was just that—an accident. Nobody's fault, no guilt to carry around. Yes, it had changed things. But I was getting used to changes, including starting at a new school in Rio Vista this fall. No one there could compare the Before me and After me. And even if they stared at me, what did I care?

I knew I wasn't the helpless invalid they might think I was. That would be my little secret. And having a good secret made me feel powerful. What was it Gran used to say? *Saber es poder.* Knowledge is power. At last, I knew just what she'd meant.